THE GIRL FROM THE QUEEN'S HEAD

LINDSEY HUTCHINSON

B

Boldwood

First published in Great Britain in 2026 by Boldwood Books Ltd.

Cover Design by Head Design Ltd.

Cover Images: Shutterstock and iStock

A CIP catalogue record for this book is available from the British Library.

Paperback ISBN 978-1-83518-929-0

Large Print ISBN 978-1-83518-930-6

Hardback ISBN 978-1-83518-928-3

Trade Paperback ISBN 978-1-80656-317-3

Ebook ISBN 978-1-83518-931-3

Kindle ISBN 978-1-83518-932-0

Audio CD ISBN 978-1-83518-923-8

MP3 CD ISBN 978-1-83518-924-5

Digital audio download ISBN 978-1-83518-926-9

This book is printed on certified sustainable paper. Boldwood Books is dedicated to putting sustainability at the heart of our business. For more information please visit https://www.boldwoodbooks.com/about-us/sustainability/

Boldwood Books Ltd, 23 Bowerdean Street, London, SW6 3TN

www.boldwoodbooks.com

1

1889

'What was it for this time, Jess?' Peg Butler asked as she bathed her friend's cut lip.

Jess Lacey winced as the cold water stung. Her left eye was swollen and almost closed and a dribble of blood ran from her nose. 'Same as usual,' Jess said while Peg soaked the cloth then wrung it out to gently pat Jess's bloody nose.

'You can't go on like this, love, you do know that?'

Jess nodded. 'Thanks, Peg.' She watched, through her good eye, Peg empty and wash the bowl and cloth, then set the kettle to boil.

Retaking her seat at the table, Peg went on. 'The next time he could kill you!'

'He said he was sorry...' Jess began.

'He always bloody does! He batters you senseless then comes the old *I didn't mean it* routine. Jess, he ain't never gonna change.'

'I know you're right, Peg, but what can I do? I ain't got any money and I can only cook and clean. I'd never be able to get a job even if I left.'

'Look, the first thing is getting away from Bill. Once you've done that, then you can worry about finding work.'

'Where would I go?' Jess asked, pushing her dark hair off her forehead.

'Anywhere! There's a big world out there so pick a spot and go!' Peg's blonde curls bounced as she threw out her arm and pointed to the window. 'You've lived in Brick Kiln Croft for years, but Jess – you can make a home anywhere!'

'It's easy for you to say 'cos you ain't the one leaving.' A tear formed in Jess's good eye, flooding the green iris before spilling over her lower lashes.

'I'm not the one being beaten every week by a drunken husband.'

'He can't understand why we don't have any kids...' Jess tried to explain yet again.

'Christ Almighty, give me patience!' Peg exploded. 'We've had this out before, Jess, many times. He blames you – calls you barren, when it could just as easily be him firing blanks!'

Jess smiled then winced as the cut on her lip began to bleed again.

'You're still having your monthlies?' When Jess nodded, Peg continued, 'There you go then. Stands to reason it ain't down to you. The problem is Bill, his little swimmers ain't strong enough to get the job done.'

Jess chuckled, dabbing her lip on her handkerchief. 'You are such a tonic, Peg, you do my heart good.'

'Ar, well, I still can, but from a distance. Jess, I'm begging you, please – leave Bill before it's too late!'

The two dear friends went on to have the same conversation they'd had so many times before.

'When I met Bill he was clean and tidy. He had his job as a porter on the railway and he was a charmer.'

'Yes, and after all these years he's still a porter,' Peg put in.

'I tried to persuade him to train as an engine driver, but he wouldn't go for it.'

'The extra money would have been useful,' Peg said.

Jess nodded. 'Then he started drinking with his mates after work. This is how he gets when he's in his cups.' She pointed to her face, her eye now completely closed and already beginning to turn black.

'Don't I know it. Jess, you've taken this for years now and it's time to get out and make a life for yourself away from the violence.' Peg stood to make tea.

Jess thought about her friend's words; Peg was right, of course. She knew she couldn't live in fear of her husband any longer, but she was scared to leave. How would she live and where would she go? Her nerves were frayed and she was terrified to go home, even though she only lived next door. Her hands shook as she thought about Bill coming home drunk yet again. How he would drag her upstairs and throw her on the bed where he would force himself on her. Her stomach roiled and she began to sweat. Her mouth was dry and she gulped the hot tea given to her, burning her tongue.

'When should I do it?' she asked at last.

'As soon as possible.'

'It will have to be tomorrow then after Bill goes to work.'

'Right, tell him you need housekeeping money...'

'Peg, it's only Wednesday, I don't get that until Friday!' Jess interrupted.

'Say you want to cook him summat special and you need a few bob more. Then in the morning pack a bag and go. Find somewhere to live and write to me so I can visit you.'

'Where though?'

'Don't stay in Wednesbury 'cos it would be too easy to find you if Bill has a mind to.'

'Do you think he would come looking?' Jess asked.

'Yes, I do, if only to save face in front of his cronies. He's on to a good thing with you, Jess. You cook, clean, mend, wash, shop and you provide him with a punch bag whenever he's in a temper.'

'I could catch the train...'

'What? Jess, he's a porter – he'll see you!' Peg blasted.

'Yes, of course. Oh, Peg, what am I to do then?'

'Get a cab and go to Birmingham. The place is so big now you could get lost and he would never find you. Then, if you wanted to, you could move further afield, to the seaside maybe.'

'I like the sound of that,' Jess said as she realised her shaking had ceased.

'All right, I'll be round in the morning to help you pack a bag.'

Peg looked at her friend over the rim of her teacup. Beneath the bruises she saw a lovely face, vivid green eyes surrounded by thick dark lashes. Hair so dark it appeared black always piled neatly at the back of her head. Creamy smooth skin over high cheekbones and a trim figure despite being encased in a pinafore apron.

'What?' Jess asked.

'You have a heart of gold and a soul of silver, Jess.' Seeing the girl shake her head, Peg went on. 'I recall last winter when old Mr Appleby slipped on the ice on his path. You saw him go down hard and ran to fetch me. We picked him up and took him back into the house where you wrapped him in a blanket then made him some hot sweet tea. I thought he was done for, he was so white with shock.' Jess nodded. 'For a week you took him a hot meal in the evenings before Bill came home from work, and in the mornings you went to light his fire.'

'I remember. He's such a nice old gent.'

'Like I said, you're kind and considerate and you don't deserve what Bill keeps dishing out. You have to get away, Jess, stiffen your resolve and take the plunge.'

Jess left her friend feeling anxious but excited. She had finally made up her mind to flee her abusive husband and set out to make a new life for herself. She knew it would be hard going but at least she would be free to make her own decisions. Right or wrong, she would only have herself to answer to. It was a big step to take, and she began to feel afraid as she stepped into the familiar comfort of her kitchen.

Looking around at the table and chairs, the small range and the old sink, Jess recognised she would be leaving it all behind. *They're only things*, she thought, *I can have more things once I'm settled somewhere safe.*

Feeling a tear form again in her good eye, Jess Lacey realised she hadn't let herself have a good cry in a very long time. The enormity of it all crashed in on her and, dropping onto a kitchen chair, Jess allowed the floodgates to open. She wept for all the wasted years she'd spent with a man she no longer loved. She sobbed over the beatings she had taken because she couldn't get pregnant, and she howled at having to leave Peg – her only friend in the world.

2

Bill Lacey stumbled in through the back door of the two up, two down house he shared with his wife, Jess, and staggered to a kitchen chair.

'Whatsh for tea?' he yelled.

'Stew and dumplings,' Jess replied as she sliced fresh bread. Then, gathering her courage, she went on, 'Bill, I'd like to cook you something special so...'

'Why?'

'Well, I think you deserve it because you work so hard every day.'

'Too bloody right I do!' Bill dug in his pocket. Pulling out a shilling, he slapped it on the table. 'Get some steak and make sure you cook it properly.'

Jess scooped up the coin and dropped it into her apron pocket. Then she served him his meal. Sitting to eat her own, Jess's mind was on the money Bill had handed over in such a cavalier fashion. It was a huge amount and would aid her a great deal over the following weeks. As she ate, she prayed he would go to the boozer later or, if not, he would fall asleep in the armchair. Her nerves jumped when he pushed back his seat and wove his way into the living room. She heard him muttering as he tripped, then titter when he finally made it into his armchair. With her spoon halfway to her mouth, she waited. Finally, hearing his snores, she relaxed enough to finish her food.

After washing the dishes and tidying the kitchen, Jess stole quietly through the living room and up the stairs to bed. She knew Bill wouldn't wake before the morning so she could sleep safe and well.

* * *

The next morning, Bill woke with a start. Squinting at the clock on the mantelshelf, he jumped up, immediately regretting it when his head pounded. Going to the kitchen, he said, 'I'm late! Why didn't you wake me?'

'I was cooking your breakfast,' Jess replied quietly.

'I ain't got time for that now because of you!' Bill stamped out of the house, leaving Jess staring at the plate of bacon and eggs.

'That's a shame,' she muttered before sitting down. With a smile, she devoured her husband's food.

Just as she finished washing up, Peg burst in through the back door. 'Come on, let's get at it.' Grabbing Jess by the arm, she pulled her upstairs.

Jess brought out an old cardboard suitcase from the wardrobe and shoved into it her underwear, spare stockings and garters, nightdress, toothbrush and her only other dress.

'Anything else?' Peg asked and when Jess shook her head she picked up the suitcase, saying, 'Put this under the kitchen table in case Bill comes back. Put your coat on while I hail a cab.'

The two women descended the stairs and in the kitchen Jess did as she was bid.

Out on the street, Peg yelled at a waiting cabbie. When he pulled up, she said 'Birmingham.'

'It'd be cheaper by train,' he said.

'It ain't none of your business,' Peg snapped before calling to Jess.

The cabbie winced as he saw the state of his passenger and, holding up a hand, he said, 'I know it ain't none of my business. So where in Birmingham?'

'As far away from here as possible,' Peg replied, pushing Jess and her bag into the carriage. Hugging her friend, she said, 'Write to me when you can.'

'I will.' Pulling off her wedding ring, Jess gave it to Peg. 'Sell it and keep the money for me, I might need it one day. Thanks, Peg – for everything.'

The carriage rolled away and Peg watched it disappear, tears rolling down her face.

* * *

Jess too had a little cry in the cab and then determinedly dried her eyes. She was setting out on a great new adventure and her stomach flipped with excitement. She was scared by the thought of having to fend for herself in the big city, but at least she was away from Bill. A giggle escaped her lips as she thought of him expecting steak for tea. He would be furious when he discovered there was no steak – and no Jess.

He would stamp round to Peg's, yelling to know where his wife was. Peg would tell him to get lost and her husband, Jim, a big man, would send Bill home with a flea in his ear.

Jess looked out of the window onto a bright new world and

smiled. Watching people rushing about, Jess wondered if anyone was in a similar position to hers, after all, no one really knew what went on behind closed doors. The streets were busy with folk bustling around, seemingly with places to go. Mothers with screaming babies on their hips, toffs striding out wearing top hats and swinging canes, and workers in their moleskin trousers and ragged jackets hurrying to their place of employment. Somehow she was going to become one of the anonymous people ambling about. Free at last, she felt the weight lift from her shoulders and she sent up a silent prayer that, even if he searched, Bill would never find her.

3

The cab carried Jess the eight miles to the city, the cabbie keeping the horse to a walk, knowing the beast would be working until he could rest her for the afternoon when another mare would take over, then negotiated the traffic along the busy streets which were packed with folk rushing this way and that. Carts and wagons rolled past in the other direction, and Jess heard the huffing of the steam train as they passed New Street station. Dirty buildings stood cheek by jowl and large shop windows advertised the goods to be found inside.

Jess covered her nose as the smell from the abattoir reached her, then they traversed the famous Bull Ring. In days gone by, the green within the area of Corn Cheaping was used for bull baiting. The ring was a hoop of iron to which bulls were tied before being slaughtered. Jess was glad the practice was no longer used. Through Digbeth they turned into Floodgate Street before turning again into the quieter Allcock Street. Up one road and down another, the cab kept going and Jess began to fret about where she would end up. She didn't know the area at all, with its buildings all shoved together, barely allowing a sliver of light to pass between them.

Finally the cab halted and the cabbie jumped down to open the door.

'You didn't say where to drop you, miss,' he said as he pointed to the park.

'This will do nicely.' Jess rummaged in her bag for the fare, then, thanking the cabbie, she picked up her suitcase and sauntered in through the park gates. She knew she would have to find lodgings for the night but she needed time to consider where she would go from there. Seeing a bench, Jess sat down, her case at her feet.

The cabbie watched her go and, returning to his seat, he pulled his vehicle just around the corner. Placing the feed bag over the horse's nose, letting people know he was unavailable, he then retook his seat where he could watch the young woman in the park. He had a bad feeling about all this and wanted to make sure no harm came to her. Clearly she was fleeing abuse – from her husband maybe? Pulling out his pipe, he stacked it with tobacco and lit it with a match. As he puffed, he kept a discreet eye on the girl on the bench. He was convinced she had no idea where she was, evidently she didn't know the area at all. Would she try to sleep in the park? No, she would be moved on by the park-keeper when he came to lock the gates for the night. Then where would she go? Despite needing the fares, the cabbie stayed where he was, his concern for the young woman paramount in his mind. He feared for her all alone in the city, she was vulnerable and when darkness fell she would be at risk of being attacked or robbed. For an hour the cabbie watched and waited, then, unable to help himself, he jumped down onto the pavement and walked briskly to the girl who, he now saw, was sobbing quietly.

'Pardon me, miss, but I thought you could do with a little aid.'

'Oh, thank you, but I'll be all right,' Jess said, wiping away her tears.

'Do you have anywhere to go?' he asked.

'No, but I'll find somewhere to spend the night, I'm sure.'

'Come on, my cab is just around the corner. I know of a place where you'll be safe.' Jess instinctively pulled away from the man as he held out a hand to her. 'I won't hurt you, I promise, but I can't leave you out here overnight.'

Jess nodded. Something in the man's eyes told her he was speaking the truth and that she would be all right with him.

The cabbie took her suitcase and led Jess back to his cab. Helping her inside, he said, 'Two minutes and we'll be there. I swear you'll be fine.'

True to his word, the cabbie removed the nose bag which he shoved in the box beneath his seat and climbed up. Two streets away, the cab pulled up and he again jumped down and opened the door. Jess climbed out and looked up at the building. 'A public house?' she asked, wondering what he was up to.

'I can guess what you're thinking, miss, but I promise, no harm will come to you here.' With that, the cabbie walked to a side door and hammered loudly.

Jess glanced around for a getaway route if things turned ugly, but she was surprised when a woman answered the knock.

'Hello, Ernie,' the red-headed woman said. Short and slim, she had a broad smile on her face.

'How do, Ellen. I have a lady here I think is in need of some help,' the cabbie replied.

Ellen stepped forward and gasped as she saw Jess's face. 'Oh, my dear girl. Come in, I promise all will be well. I do my best for young women who are like you.'

Jess, who instinctively tentatively trusted the woman, said, 'I have to pay my cab fare.'

'Don't worry about that, Ernie will put it on his bill for me, won't you, lad,' Ellen replied. 'Come on in and let's get you fed and settled in your own room.'

Jess thanked the cabbie, who tipped his hat before returning to his cab. Then she followed the woman inside The Queen's Head.

'I'm Ellen Marsh and you are?'

'Jess Lacey.'

'Well, Jess, welcome. You'll be safe here with us.'

Ascending the carpeted staircase, Jess was led to a room which overlooked the street. It was cosy, if small. There was a single bed, wardrobe, chest of drawers and a dressing table. It was lit by electric and Jess smiled as Ellen flicked the switch.

'Through there is what I like to call the bathroom,' Ellen said, pointing to a door. 'It is in fact a large cupboard but it has a lavvy and a sink. If you want a bath then it's down the hall. No one will disturb you up here.'

'I don't know how to thank you,' Jess mumbled, overcome at the kindness shown her. 'How much is it per night?'

'I don't want your money, Jess.'

Suddenly Jess felt uncomfortable. What was expected of her in return for board and lodging? 'Maybe I should be on my way.'

'No, no. I'm sorry, what I meant was… Look, I own this place and I'm very wealthy thanks to my late husband. The local cabbies know I try to help the less fortunate in their time of need. I'm guessing you're running away from an abusive husband?' When Jess nodded, she went on. 'You can stay here as long as you like. In return, should you wish, you could help clean the pub or serve behind the bar. There's a lock on your door and you'll have three meals a day. When you want to leave, just remember to say goodbye.'

'That's it?' Jess asked.

'Yes. There's no more to it than that.'

'I don't know how to thank you enough.'

'When you've settled in, come downstairs and meet the others.'

'Others?' Jess asked.

'Yes. We do run a pub so we need kitchen and bar staff, cleaners and cellar workers.'

'Of course, I wasn't thinking.'

'You'll be fine, take your time.' With that, Ellen left Jess to unpack the few things she had.

Jess had a look around her lodgings, hardly able to believe she had her own indoor privy! Glancing out of the window, she saw people coming and going and, although still a little afraid, she was also excited.

Hanging up her dress and placing her underwear and stockings in a drawer, she sat on the bed. She wanted to go downstairs to meet everyone but she was scared. Something was telling her there was more to it here than just aiding the poor and helpless. Then again, she couldn't hide in her room forever. Getting to her feet, Jess took the first steps that would lead her into a whole new life.

4

At the bottom of the stairs, Jess looked around. Seeing a door, she pushed it open a crack and peeped through. It led directly to the bar so she tried the door opposite – the kitchen. *That's better*, she thought and walked in.

'Hello, you new?' a girl asked. Jess nodded. 'I'm Gail Henley, nice to meet you.' Gail had auburn hair and large eyes that sparkled as she smiled. Quite tall, she moved with the grace of a dancer around the kitchen.

'You too. I'm Jess Lacey.' The friendly girl said nothing about the state of her face, and for that Jess was grateful.

'I'm the cook. Are you hungry?' Without waiting for an answer, Gail plated up sausages, mash and vegetables in onion gravy. 'Sit and I'll brew up.'

Jess found a seat at the table which was set with cutlery and began to eat. Tea was delivered by Gail, who smiled then went back to her stove.

A little later, Ellen came through to join them. 'I'm so glad you're eating.'

'It was delicious,' Jess replied, laying her cutlery on the empty plate.

'So, you've met Gail. She's a marvel, I don't know how we'd manage without her. Come through to the bar and meet Carol Potts. She's our barmaid. Very quiet is Carol, she's not very sociable. She's not been here long.'

Jess and Carol were introduced and Jess saw what Ellen meant. The poor girl seemed frightened, getting on with her work but saying little.

'Oh, and here's Carter Adams, he's our cellar man.'

The handsome young man smiled a warm welcome and shook Jess's hand. His dark hair fell over light brown eyes and Jess immediately felt shy. His bulging muscles were a testament to hauling casks and barrels around, both in the cellar and out in the yard. As she looked up at him, Jess felt a tingle in her stomach and her heart began to pound.

'Are you going to be helping Carol in the bar then?' he asked. It had taken him a moment to compose himself at the sight of the beautiful girl beneath her bruises.

'I don't know anything about bar work,' Jess said timidly.

'It's easy,' Carol put in quietly. 'I'll show you.'

'All right, thank you.'

Ellen and Carter went to the kitchen for lunch and Jess's lesson in pulling pints began. She was shown how to tip the glass until it was almost full then level it up. Carol instructed her in the use of the till and where the glasses and spirits were kept, as well as how to measure the amounts.

Jess was a natural and inside an hour it was like she'd been there all her life. She laughed and joked with the customers, all the while relieving them of their money.

Ellen and Carter stood in the doorway watching, hardly able to believe their eyes.

'That's a nice shiner you've got there,' a fellow said.

Ellen grinned when Jess came back with, 'You mind I don't give you one to match.'

Laughter filled the bar as his mates patted the man's back in consolation at being outdone by the new girl.

Jess was on her feet well into the evening, only breaking for a meal, and wasn't aware she was tired until closing time.

'Well done,' Carol said blandly, then disappeared to her room.

Jess dried the last of the glasses and went to the kitchen.

'Cuppa?' Gail asked.

'Oh, yes, please!'

The two sat to drink their tea, both weary after working so hard. They began to talk and before long Jess felt comfortable to open up as she related her tale of escaping a violent husband.

'I can't even imagine what you've been through, but you're safe now,' Gail said. 'I love to cook and I've been here ten years.'

'I was a bit dubious when I first arrived, I must admit. I thought I'd be expected to...'

'Yes, I know, all the girls think that when they come here. I don't think Ellen explains herself very well.' They shared a little laugh and Gail went on. 'You will be looked after here so please don't worry.'

'Do the girls move on after a while then?' Jess asked.

'Yes, usually. They save their wages and then they're gone.'

'Wages?'

'Yes. Bloody hell, Ellen! Clearly she didn't tell you that you'll be paid for any work you do.'

'No, she forgot that part.' Again they laughed and Jess felt she could well have made another close friend.

* * *

Whilst Jess had been enjoying her new job, back in Wednesbury her drunken husband had railed loudly at having no wife – or steak for tea. Bill had banged on Peg's door, yelling at the top of his voice, 'Where is she? Where's my bloody wife?'

'I don't know,' Peg answered truthfully.

'Yesh, you do! You tell me or else!'

'Bill, I don't know. Now go home and sleep off the beer,' Peg said.

'I know you know where she is, Peg Butler...' Bill waved a finger at her and howled in pain when Jim Butler stepped up and twisted it.

'If my wife says she doesn't know then you'd best believe her.'

'All right, Jimbo, no need to get riled up,' Bill said, swaying from foot to foot.

'Don't call me Jimbo. Now bugger off and leave us in peace.' Jim slammed the door in Bill's face.

Turning carefully, Bill walked down the path, climbed over the little gate and up his own path. He could be heard all down the street as he cussed his wife whilst he searched the cupboards for something to eat.

'Stole my shilling, she did! Took her hook and left me; didn't even cook my tea! Bloody woman, you wait 'til I find you. I'll tan yer arse, you see if I don't!'

For half an hour, Bill banged around in the kitchen before he gave up and tottered to his armchair. There he muttered for another ten minutes before silence fell. Bill Lacey was out for the count.

5

Jess went to her bedroom and locked her door. She washed and lay listening to the sounds of the street; women's laughter, men singing as they wove their way home, cabs rolling over the cobblestones. All the while she was dreading hearing Bill banging on the doors shouting her name.

Eventually sleep claimed her and she woke refreshed, and glad that her fears had not come true. She was here in Birmingham and she almost wept with relief. Washed and dressed, she went downstairs where she was greeted by Gail holding out a cup of coffee.

'How did you sleep?' Gail asked.

'Like a baby – in the end. It took me a while to go off.'

'Understandably, but now you know you're safe and welcome here it should get easier.'

'Thanks, Gail, I appreciate it.'

'Right, breakfast. They'll all be in shortly wanting to be fed.'

'Can I help?' Jess asked.

'You can, you're frying eggs,' Gail said with a grin.

Jess set the large frying pan on the hotplate and dropped in a knob of lard. 'How many do we need?' she asked.

'Two each. You, me, Ellen, Carol, Carter and Kathy the cleaner.'

'Twelve it is then,' Jess said.

The aroma of bacon drifted up the stairs and soon brought hungry people to the kitchen. Everyone sat around the huge table and enjoyed their food.

Jess met Kathy Frith for the first time and was surprised. She thought at first she was an older woman, but on closer inspection she realised they were around the same age. Kathy wore a constant frown and grumbled under her breath a lot.

When they had all finished, Jess stayed to help with the washing up. Carol went to stock the bar, Kathy to sweep and mop the floor, Ellen to her office and Carter to the cellar.

'I wonder if I could borrow a pen and paper, I need to let my friend know where I am,' Jess said as she dried the last plate.

'I wouldn't if I were you,' Gail advised. 'It might be better to start afresh, cut all ties to your old life.'

'I can't do that to Peg. She's been my only friend for years.'

'What if your old man finds out...?'

'Peg wouldn't tell him!' Jess interrupted. 'I'm sorry, I didn't mean to be so sharp.' Gail smiled and Jess continued. 'Peg would never divulge my whereabouts, she's nursed my wounds too often.'

'If you're sure then Ellen can provide what you need. Just tell your friend to burn the letter after she reads it because you never know.'

'I will, thank you.' Jess went in search of Ellen with her request. Her benefactor also warned against sending a letter but Jess was adamant so Ellen gave in. Jess went to her room to write to Peg. An hour later, she was behind the bar once more and was astonished at the amount of people pouring through the doors.

Ten o'clock in the morning and men were on the ale and women were drinking gin like they were dying of thirst. Jess wondered where they got their money from as none appeared to work. She asked Carol quietly and the reply came with a shrug. 'They're probably burglars or thieves.'

Jess couldn't help but smile because it made sense. Steal at night and spend the pelf the next day once they'd hocked the goods. She had no more time to dwell on it as folk were calling for service. All morning she pulled pints and measured out spirits. The bar was noisy as people talked, argued and laughed loudly. Fresh sawdust on the floor soaked up spills, and cigarette smoke swirled, turning the air grey. The electric lights attached to the walls lit up the room well, adding to the meagre daylight coming in through the small bullion windows. Along the back wall the long highly polished counter held the beer pumps and at the end was a lift-up section with a small gate for access to the corridor leading to the kitchen. Beneath the counter were glasses of all sizes and bottles of spirits.

Carter took a turn behind the bar while Jess and Carol went to the kitchen to eat lunch.

'You seem to be fitting in well,' Ellen said as Jess sat at the table.

'Too well,' Kathy muttered, but was ignored, something Jess had already noticed seemed to be the standard response to Kathy's grumblings.

'I'm enjoying it,' Jess admitted. 'Everyone here is so nice.'

'One big happy family,' Gail called over her shoulder.

'What's your story then?' Kathy Frith asked.

'Now, Kathy, you know we don't ask questions of our new

arrivals. If Jess wishes to tell us, she will do so in her own good time.'

Ellen's gentle reprimand made Kathy scowl. She shrugged her shoulders, saying, 'I was only trying to be friendly.'

'My husband did this to me.' Jess pointed to her black eye where the swelling had already gone down quite a lot. 'So I left him.'

'Bloody men!' Kathy mumbled.

'No woman should have to put up with that kind of treatment,' Gail added.

'I agree,' Ellen put in. 'That's why we do what we can to help.'

'How did the cabbie know to bring me here?' Jess asked.

'Because he's my brother. He cabs Wednesbury and Birmingham and spreads the word to his cabbie pals.'

'You said my fare would be put on his bill.'

'Yes. I pay the fare whenever they bring someone here. That way we save another soul and the cabbie gets paid.'

'What if they give the game away?'

'They don't, I make sure they receive a good tip so it's worth their while to keep our secrets,' Ellen explained.

'Pardon my asking but how do you finance it all?'

'She's rich,' Carol said.

'Indeed.' Ellen smiled. 'As well as the money my late husband left me, this place makes a tidy profit and I have my fingers in a good many pies.'

'So that's how you can pay everyone for their work,' Jess said.

'You're a bright one, ain't yer?' Kathy said quietly.

'Forgive Kathy, she likes to be sarcastic as well as moan about everything,' Ellen said with a grin.

Kathy rolled her eyes and stood to take her empty plate to the sink. 'I'll start upstairs.'

'Each day she cleans a part of the pub, then she sits in the bar,' Ellen informed Jess. 'She'll give your room a go over but don't worry, she won't touch your things.'

'I have nothing but a dress and some underwear, so I'm not concerned.'

'I'm out this afternoon, I have a meeting at the Crown and Cushion, but I'll see you later,' Ellen called as she left the kitchen.

'She owns that pub as well as this one, the Old Red Lion and The King's Head,' Gail explained.

'Good grief, that must keep her busy,' Jess said.

'She puts managers in to run each one so she only has to keep an eye on things.'

'Do they all take in...?' Jess ventured.

'The less fortunate? Yes, Ellen runs all her pubs the same. She's been doing it for years and so far it's worked well.'

Taking her plate to the sink, Jess washed it and set it aside to drain. 'Thanks, Gail, that was really good. I'll be off back to the bar.'

As she walked behind the counter, Jess heard Carter say, 'Ah, here she is, folks, our Jess.'

'About time, I don't want to see his ugly mush. I like summat pretty to look at when I'm 'aving a beer!' a customer called out.

'See what I have to put up with?' Carter asked with a grin. 'But I have to agree with him.'

Jess blushed at the compliment and lowered her eyes. 'I'd best get on.'

Carter's grin widened. 'Good luck, they're rowdy today.' He left her then to have his own lunch.

A man banged a coin on the counter and Jess eyed him. 'Another beer here.'

'Did your mother not teach you any manners?' Jess called back as she continued to fill a glass.

'Cheeky young chit,' the man said. 'Just get over here and bring me a beer!'

A feeling of fear crept over Jess; it was like being back home with Bill ordering her about. Peg's voice floated through her mind. *Tell him to bugger off!*

Straightening her back, she said, 'I'll be with you in just a moment, sir.'

'Now, woman! I'm thirsty!'

'Oh, well, in that case...' Jess poured half a glass of beer and placed it before the man.

'What the...? What's this?' he asked, glancing at the drink.

'I didn't think you could wait long enough for me to fill it to the top as you are so thirsty.' Jess suddenly realised that the bar had gone quiet and all ears were on the exchange.

'Just fill it and do it now!' the man yelled.

Jess picked up the glass, unaware that Gail and Carter were watching from the doorway. Leaning forward as if she was going to whisper to him, Jess poured the beer over his head and stood back as applause broke out. Cheers and whistles rang loud as the man stared angrily at Jess. Then he launched himself forward, grabbing Jess's dress and dragging her towards him. 'You bitch!' he growled.

In an instant, Carter was by her side, chopping his hand down on the man's arm, making him release Jess. 'Okay, pal, let's be having you outside to cool off.' Carter virtually carried the man out of the pub. On the street he said, 'Don't come back, you're not welcome here.' He watched with a smile as the man marched away.

Back indoors, he said to Jess, 'That wasn't very wise, he could have really hurt you.'

'Thanks for your help, but I'm sick to death of being spoken to like I'm a slave!' Jess's voice carried over the noise of the bar. 'I am not a skivvy! I am a woman and I have a right to live free of fear!'

Again applause rang out and Jess looked at the customers who were clapping for her. Turning back to Carter, she saw him smiling broadly, and then she laughed. For the first time in years, Jess Lacey laughed until her sides ached.

6

A couple of days later, Peg Butler excitedly tore open the letter, already knowing it was from Jess; no one else would write to her. She read the contents with a smile spreading across her face. Her friend was safe at last. Taking note of the address, she threw the letter in the fire and watched it burn. Then she sat to write to Jess, saying she would visit but not for a while. She didn't want to risk Bill following her should he have a mind to. She told of Bill's drunken yelling and how Jim had sent him packing before catching her friend up with her own news. Once the letter was finished, she went to town to post it and do some shopping. She would tell her husband later that Jess was safe, knowing he would never divulge Jess's whereabouts.

As she strolled down the path, Peg was unaware of the eyes watching her from next door.

Bill Lacey was too drunk to go to work and stood swaying by the window. 'You know where she is,' he muttered as Peg disappeared down the street. 'You can pretend you don't, but I know better.' Dropping into his armchair, Bill tried to focus his thoughts. Too drunk to think straight, however, in the end he gave up, slumped into his armchair and promptly fell asleep.

* * *

Over in Birmingham, Jess was relishing her new life.

'When are you gonna give me a kiss?' an old fellow asked as she passed him his beer.

'When you start putting your teeth in,' Jess replied with a wink.

'You don't stand a chance, old fella,' another said, 'not while young Carter is around.'

Jess smiled and shook her head as the two burst out laughing. She could feel Carter's eyes on her from the doorway but resisted turning around.

'Jess, love, give us another before we go to work,' a woman said.

Jess measured two gins, placed them on the counter and took the money. She knew the women in question would be walking the streets very shortly. She liked them both enormously, not standing in judgement of their choice of profession. It was only by the grace of God that she was not doing the same in order to survive.

'Ta, lovey,' Bella said. Turning to her friend, she said, 'I don't want to go out there tonight, Enid.'

'I know, but we have to earn a coin, otherwise we can't have a gin or two,' Enid replied.

Jess leaned on the counter and listened in. Bella was tall and built more like a man than a woman. Her dark hair was piled up untidily with wisps escaping the pins meant to hold it in place. She had a square jaw and a loud voice. She was known for speaking her mind and not caring a jot who heard her. In contrast, Enid was short, around five feet three inches, and very slim. She had masses of unruly blonde hair and her laugh was more of a cackle.

'I could do with a job like our Jess here,' Bella said before taking a sip.

'Ar, me an' all, but jobs are rare as rocking horse shit.'

Jess laughed at Enid's statement.

'Enid, you have such a foul bloody mouth,' Bella said before howling at her own joke.

Jess left them to serve another customer and when she turned back, the women had gone. They would be heading home to change their clothes and apply the thick make-up synonymous with their chosen profession, probably share another few drinks there before night closed in and they would set out to stand their pitch. With a sigh, Jess collected their glasses and washed them up.

'Go and get a sit down and a cuppa,' Carter said, 'I'll take over for a while.'

'Thanks,' Jess replied gratefully. Sitting in the kitchen, Jess felt eyes on her and when she looked up, Kathy was staring at her. Jess smiled to cover her discomfort but Kathy just looked away so Jess dismissed it as Kathy just being her grumpy self. Then Kathy headed off to her usual seat in the bar where she would spend the evening, gin in hand.

After a hot cup of tea and twenty minutes with her feet up, Jess felt refreshed enough to return to the bar. Carol took her break, leaving Jess to work alongside Carter.

They were a team made in heaven as they manoeuvred around each other, keeping the customers happy.

'Gin? Certainly,' Jess said loudly and was shocked when Carter slid the bottle along the counter. Catching it deftly, she poured the drink and took payment. 'Coming back!' she called, mimicking Carter's antics with the bottle.

Cheers rang out as he caught it and then flipped a glass in the air before filling it. Jess laughed loudly before doing the same, enjoying how much the customers were loving the spectacle.

The hours fled past and before she knew it, it was locking-up time.

'That was fun,' Jess said as she and Carter went to the kitchen.

'It was,' Carter replied with a smile.

'What happened to Carol?' Jess asked, only now realising the girl had not returned from her break.

'She's gone,' Gail informed her.

'Gone? Where to?' Jess asked, surprise written all over her face.

'Who knows? It happens. She just said she was leaving and then poof – she disappeared.'

'Isn't that rather sudden? Oh dear, I hope it wasn't because of me,' Jess said, wondering if she had driven the girl away.

'No, it wasn't,' Gail reassured her. 'She's been saying for a while that she was ready to move on.'

Jess felt relieved at not being the reason Carol had gone. 'We'll be short in the bar now though.'

Ellen made them all jump as she came in, saying, 'Not if Carter works with you. It was amazing out there tonight, you two are great together.'

'I'd like that, and I can still do the cellar work,' Carter said.

Jess nodded. 'You will have to think up some more tricks then.'

'I've not seen the bar so full in a long time, I think word of our new barmaid is getting around,' Ellen smiled.

A look of worry passed over Jess's face as she considered how far that word could travel, and whether Bill would hear of it.

Over tea they chatted about the success of Ellen's pubs before finally drifting away to their beds.

Ablutions completed, Jess lay in bed, watching the moonbeams dance across the ceiling. A barking dog gave a yelp, then went silent. Slowly the sounds of the street receded until all was quiet once more. Thinking about the evening's escapades, Jess smiled in the darkness. Carter Adams really was a nice man. He made her laugh, but more importantly he made her feel safe. It didn't hurt that he was handsome either. Jess felt the heat rise to her cheeks as she pictured him in her mind. Was she developing feelings for this man? Her head said no, she mustn't allow it, but her heart was telling her different.

You mustn't get involved, she told herself. *You are a married woman still, despite being separated.* She didn't want to drag Carter into the whole sordid affair of her abusive marriage. What would happen if Bill *did* find out where she was and came looking for her? It wouldn't be fair on Carter or herself. No, it was better for both of them that they remain friends. But despite making that decision, Jess couldn't help but wonder how it would feel to be held by the good-looking Mr Adams.

7

Over the coming days, Jess found she could manage the bar alone during the daytime, and in the evenings Carter joined her when it was really busy.

Sliding bottles, tossing and flipping glasses had the customers cheering loudly. Each night the bar was busier than the previous one and Jess was loving it. She was born to be a barmaid. She couldn't deny their antics were bringing in more custom and she revelled in the joy of it all. Her battered face had healed nicely and her green eyes sparkled like emeralds as she laughed with the punters.

'We only come in here to see you,' a retired army officer said one evening. 'Isn't that right, chaps?'

A cheer went up, as did glasses in salute.

'I should think so too. Where else would you find a lovelier lady?' Carter yelled over the melee.

'It seems you have an admirer if I'm not mistaken, young lady,' the officer said before tipping back his whisky.

'What can I say? You either have it or you don't,' Jess replied with a grin.

'Oh, yes, rather! Fill her up again, if you would, m'dear.'

Jess pondered the officer's words as she went about her business. She was glad that Carter did indeed seem to like her, but she still felt it was safer that they stay as friends. Nobody noticed Kathy sitting with a look on her face that could sour milk.

* * *

The following morning, Jess finally received Peg's letter and she was overjoyed. Reading the words, she was sorry Bill was pestering her friend, but she didn't worry too much because she knew that Jim would protect his wife should the need arise. She was excited at the thought of Peg visiting but saw the need for caution. She decided to write back during her afternoon break and tell Peg all about how well she was doing.

* * *

Eight miles away, Bill Lacey slouched in his chair. Often too drunk to work, he had finally been sacked and now he had no money coming in. If he wanted his beloved beer he would have to find a way to earn a few coins. Either that or go out on the rob. In the meantime, however, he had begun to sell off the furniture.

Peg watched people coming then going away with a chair or the settee, and she knew the reason. Out-of-work Bill needed beer money. She wondered what he would do once everything had been sold. *He needn't come begging here*, she thought as she saw him stride down the path. *There he goes – off to the pub again.*

Peg took the opportunity to go outside to wash her windows in peace. Every time she stepped foot outdoors, Bill came out too, yelling for her to tell him where Jess was. Jim had warned Bill to leave his wife alone once before, but Jim was at work during the day and her neighbour took full advantage of that fact. Bill was making her life hell and she determined she would have to tell Jim what was happening. She couldn't go on hiding it; she wouldn't let an inebriated neighbour cow her any longer.

That evening, Peg opened up to her husband about Bill harassing her and of course Jim was furious.

'He's been in the pub all day and he's not back yet,' she said.

'Leave it with me, sweetheart, I'll sort it out tomorrow,' Jim said, giving his wife a hug.

'I don't want any fighting,' Peg pleaded.

'I know. I just want to explain to him once and for all that we don't know where Jess is.'

'But we do,' Peg said.

'Yes, but he doesn't know that, and we're not going to tell him.'

Peg nodded, enjoying Jim's strong arms around her.

* * *

Early the following day, Jim hammered on Bill's door. It took a while but eventually it was opened. 'Jim! Come on in, pal.'

Jim stepped in and was shocked at what he saw. The only piece of furniture left was Bill's armchair. 'What's going on, Bill?' he asked as he glanced around.

From the lone chair, Bill said, 'Oh, I just fancied a change.' He laughed and Jim realised he was still drunk from the night before.

'Look, I'm here to tell you we don't know where Jess is so stop harassing Peg.'

'I ain't!' Bill protested.

'You are. Every time she goes out you're at her and it's got to stop!'

'I just want to...'

'I know, but I'm warning you for the last time, Bill. Leave Peg alone or I'll lamp you into next week!'

Bill held up his hands in surrender, a silly grin on his face.

Confident that the other man had got the message, Jim stormed out, slamming the door behind him.

'Touchy, ain't we?' Bill muttered at his neighbour's back, then laughed.

Before he went off to work, Jim assured Peg all would be well now.

Peg, for her part, wasn't so sure, but time would tell.

* * *

The next couple of weeks proved Jim correct as Peg came and went without Bill accosting her. Each day Bill went off to the pub and returned as drunk as a lord and Peg couldn't help wondering where the money was coming from now there was nothing left to sell.

Then, in the early hours one morning, Peg heard a noise outside. Carefully, she got out of bed and looked through the window. She saw Bill pushing a bicycle down the path and she knew – he'd stolen it. Now he was going to sell it for beer money. Peg went back to bed but couldn't sleep. She thought about Jim's tools in their shed and fretted Bill might steal them too.

Over breakfast, she told Jim what she'd seen and her fears for his belongings.

'He won't break the lock on the shed, it's too strong so don't worry about it,' Jim said.

That afternoon, Bill came home with an empty hand cart

which he pulled up the path as bold as brass. He left it at the side of the house in full view of anyone passing by. Peg was intrigued; she felt sure he had stolen it. She stayed indoors to see what would happen. Sure enough, an hour later a man came for the cart, openly paying Bill in the garden.

'Well, I never! You've got a nerve, Bill Lacey!' Peg muttered as she watched from the window. She considered telling Jess in one of her letters but she thought again. Jess was better off not knowing; let her enjoy her new life without any reminders about her old one and her useless husband.

8

Jess was indeed reaping the benefits of being away from Bill. Her confidence had soared and she felt like a different woman. From her wages she had invested in a couple of new dresses and a comfortable pair of shoes. Her dark hair shone and her emerald eyes sparkled. She laughed all the time, much to the delight of the customers.

From the sidelines Kathy Frith watched, green with envy. She had long since set her sights on Carter as a potential husband, and now this Jess Lacey had arrived and stolen Carter's attention. Kathy couldn't deny the girl was beautiful, which only made her feel more wretched. Jess could charm the birds from the trees with her winning ways, but Kathy was determined that Carter Adams would be hers eventually. All she needed was an opportunity to get rid of Jess. She would bide her time; after all, patience was a virtue.

In the early hours, a few mornings later, everyone was roused from their beds by heavy hammering on the pub doors. Carter was first down and opened up to find Bella on the doorstep in tears.

Jess was terrified, convinced Bill had finally found her; she was relieved to hear Bella's voice.

'Oh, Carter! I can't find Enid, she's gone missing!' Bella wailed.

'Come in, sit down and tell me from the beginning,' Carter said, handing Bella to Jess as he locked the doors again.

They all gathered to hear the tale.

'We went out... oh, ta.' Bella gratefully accepted a gin from Ellen. 'We were out as usual on the corner of Glover Street by the vinegar brewery. Well, this fella asks Enid, "How much?" Once they'd agreed terms, they sauntered off down the road towards the canal basin and I ain't seen her since!'

'What time was this?' Carter asked.

'Midnight, I remember the church clock striking.'

'Two hours ago,' Carter said, glancing at the clock on the wall over the bar. 'Right, I'll get dressed and go and look for her.'

'I'm coming with you,' Jess said.

Carter tried to persuade Jess it wasn't safe for her to be out so late, but once it was clear she wasn't going to change her mind, the two raced upstairs to dress before Carter ran to the scullery. From a shelf he pulled out a large lantern and a box of Swan Vestas matches.

Outside he struck a match and lit the wick, then held it up high to light their way.

Jess was right by his side and she smiled when he grabbed her hand and they ran towards the basin. Walking the towpath, Carter swung the torch around, searching the shadows.

'Enid!' Jess yelled. 'Enid!'

Both called again and again as they slowly walked along.

'Where could she have gone?' Jess asked.

'God knows. She might not be around here at all.'

Jess almost jumped out of her skin as a cat leapt out from a heap of rubbish with a yowl. 'Good grief!' she gasped, moving closer to Carter. 'It's eerie here at night.'

'There are no boats moored up where normally there would be two or three,' he replied. 'Be careful where you tread, stay away from the canal.'

'Carter, you don't think she could be in there, do you?' Jess shivered at the thought of Enid having fallen, or been pushed, into the murky dark ribbon of water.

'I doubt it. Come on, let's go further, the towpath goes right to the end.'

There were huge buildings on one side of the basin and Jess said, 'Let's look around here before we move on.'

They found nothing by the first building, then they came to an alley of sorts; a thin slice of land separating the properties.

'Enid!' Jess yelled as they peered into the darkness beyond the flare of the lantern.

'She's not there,' Carter said as he turned away.

'We have to check, she could be unconscious,' Jess pleaded.

'All right, come on.'

Slowly they stepped into the narrow space. 'Carter, look! There at the end,' Jess said. In the glow of the torch, they saw what looked like a bundle of old clothes. 'Enid?' Jess called. They heard a moan and hurried forward. 'Oh my God! Enid, we're here,' Jess said as she tried to help the woman to stand. Enid's body had other ideas though and crumpled to the ground once more.

'Here, take this,' Carter said, thrusting the lamp into Jess's hand. Then he gently lifted Enid into his arms. 'Come on, lady, let's get a gin into you at the pub.'

Enid smiled before passing out.

Jess led the way back, lighting Carter's path so he didn't stumble. By the time they arrived at the pub, Enid was awake and crying. Jess blew out the lantern and followed them indoors where Carter sat Enid on a chair in the kitchen and Gail provided hot sweet tea.

'He promised me a gin,' Enid managed between sobs.

'Tea first,' Ellen encouraged.

Bella hugged Carter, thanking him profusely for finding her friend. 'Aghh,' Carter managed, 'you're crushing me.' Bella was a big woman and really didn't know her own strength. She let him go with an apology.

Each with a cup of tea, they waited for Enid to collect herself. 'Thanks, you two,' she said at last to Carter and Jess.

'Are you up to telling us what happened?' Ellen asked.

'I saw you go off with that bloke,' Bella put in.

'Yes, I did. I thought he was a trick but it turned out he wanted more than a... he was after something quite different.'

'You shouldn't be out there,' Kathy said. She was not surprised when she was ignored by the others yet again.

'Bloody hell! Where's your whistle?' Bella demanded to know.

'I forgot it,' Enid admitted.

Puzzled by the question, Jess asked, 'Whistle?'

'Yes, all the girls carry one. That way if there's trouble they can blow for help. We're always close enough to each other to hear it.'

'Except for tonight,' Kathy muttered.

'Sensible,' Jess commented after glaring at Kathy.

'Until you forget it!' Bella boomed. Instantly she regretted her temper when Enid began to cry again. 'I'm sorry, wench. It's just... well, look at you, banged all to hell.'

'I'm all right,' Enid sobbed.

'Let me look at you properly,' Jess insisted. She checked for broken bones and found none. 'Bruising only, you were very lucky.'

'Lucky? Look at her!' Bella said sharply.

'Bella, she could have been killed! So yes, she's bloody lucky!' Jess countered.

'Oh, Jess love, I'm sorry. I'm just so upset,' Bella said. Turning to Enid, she went on. 'See what you made me do? It's all your fault. I'll nail that whistle to your hand, I swear.'

Titters sounded as the friends hugged, Enid wincing in pain as Bella held her tight.

'Do you know the punter – I mean have you seen him before?' Bella asked.

'No, he seemed nice; not from round here though. He had an accent of some sort,' Enid replied.

'What sort of accent?' Bella asked frustratedly.

'I ain't sure, Scottish – or Irish.'

Bella sighed. 'Right, I'll pass the word to the others to be on the lookout. We don't want this happening again.'

'I'll be off work for a couple of days so what about the rent?' Enid asked.

'We'll manage,' Bella assured her. To the others she explained, 'We share a house in Keeley Street. We don't take our tricks there 'cos it's our home.'

Jess nodded. 'I have a little from my wages if you're short.'

Ellen and Carter exchanged a look which said *what a lovely gesture.*

Kathy curled her lip, thinking, *Miss goody two shoes!*

'It's all right, bab, but thanks anyway.'

Jess smiled. 'Put a cold compress on that eye when you get home. I've had enough black eyes in my time to know what works.' Jess had spoken without thinking and only realised what she'd said when she saw everyone staring at her. 'My husband,' she said by way of explanation, reaffirming what they already knew, but her eyes were on Carter. She saw his face fall at finding out she was a married woman and she felt wretched.

'Come on, I'll see you ladies home,' he said.

Everyone went to bed except Jess, who had decided to wait for Carter to return. They had some talking to do.

9

'I thought you'd be in bed,' Carter said, walking into the kitchen and bolting the door top and bottom and turning the key in the lock.

'I was waiting for you. I wanted to say... thank you for finding Enid.' Jess had resolved to tell him about her life before meeting him, especially as she had suspicions he had developed feelings for her. However, now she was faced with it she couldn't do it. What if she was wrong? Maybe he was only being kind and had not set his sights on her. Then she would feel a fool and working with him would be awkward.

'I'm glad we did find her safe and well, apart from the bruises, that is.' He sighed loudly and rubbed his eyes. 'I'm tired now. I'll see you in the morning.' Carter left Jess alone in the kitchen.

After a moment, she turned off the light and went to bed, convinced now that she had been worrying about nothing. Carter was simply a very kind man and had no designs on her.

In his room, Carter peeled off his clothes and crawled into bed. What a night. Enid had gone missing after some swine had punched her senseless, and Jess had confessed she was married. She hadn't been wearing a wedding ring so he had concluded, wrongly, that she was single. Laying an arm over his eyes, Carter conjured her image and felt the sting of pain in his chest. He had fallen for Jess and knowing he couldn't have her was breaking his heart. He was certain she felt the same about him but had said nothing about a husband until now. Why hadn't she told him? From what she'd said about the black eyes, it was clear her husband wasn't good enough for her. Then again, it was none of his business; her life was her own. All he could do now was to love her from afar because no matter what, they could never be together.

In her own room, Jess was thinking much the same thing. She would have to keep her emotions to herself now she realised Carter didn't care for her the same way she cared about him. She would get on with her work and push all other feelings aside. She would have to, otherwise she would have to leave. And the thought of that scared her witless; there was nowhere else to go.

* * *

Over the weeks that followed, Jess managed to keep her feelings to herself and slowly began to venture out a little more in the spring sunshine. She went to the market with Gail and Jess relished the firm friendship that had formed between the two of them. Meandering between the market stalls, they chatted all the time, hardly hearing the calls of the traders advertising their wares. Barrow boys pushed amongst the throngs of people, shouting, 'Coming through!' The smell of fish was pungent on the air before giving way to the aroma of freshly baked bread. Further along was a cart filled with flowers, the heady fragrance floating on the gentle breeze. The two women enjoyed shopping for clothes together and even went to the music hall on a rare night off. Jess continued to work alongside Carter in the evenings which she still enjoyed enormously, despite her feelings of warmth towards him.

One balmy night, when The Queen's Head was packed to the rafters, a fellow began to sing. His voice was pure and sweet and slowly everyone hushed to listen to him. The refrain of 'If You Were Only Mine' sailed across the crowded bar and Jess realised she and Carter were staring at each other. Heat flooded her cheeks as she tore her gaze away but Carter could not do the same.

The applause was loud when the singer finished and the punters shouted for more. The young man held up his hands and yelled, 'Only if Jess will join me.'

Jess shook her head as she watched the man sidle up to the counter.

'Albert Flint at your service, but my friends call me Al. Won't you sing with me, pretty lady?'

'No, I don't think so,' Jess said with a little laugh.

Carter edged his way to stand next to Jess in a protective manner.

'One song and I promise to let you be,' Al coaxed.

The customers clamoured for her to sing, clapping and chanting her name. Kathy, sitting at the end of the bar, rolled her eyes and sipped her gin, dislike written all over her face.

Jess held up her index finger teasingly and the crowd cheered.

'"If You Were the Only Girl in the World"?' Al asked and Jess nodded.

A hush fell on the room as Al began then Jess took over before they finished together. The applause almost raised the roof. Loud whistles rang around the room and everyone shouted for more. Jess held up her hands and shook her head, and slowly the customers quietened down, albeit disappointed that she wouldn't sing again.

'You have a beautiful voice, Jess, you should be on the boards,' Al said.

'Yes, sweeping them,' came her reply and they both laughed heartily.

Carter watched this exchange, green with jealousy.

'Give us another song, Jess,' someone called out.

'And who would fill your glasses?' she replied as she moved away back to the bar to serve, unaware that both Carter and Al had eyes only for her.

As the night wore on, Al watched the girl behind the bar, and in turn Carter watched him. As far as Carter was concerned, the man was paying entirely too much attention to Jess, and he didn't like it one bit. He knew he had no right to feel as he did but he couldn't help himself. One doesn't choose who to fall in love with, he told himself and he determined he would be keeping an eye on Jess, but even more so on Al.

That night, Jess and Gail, as they often did, sat up talking long after everyone else was in bed. 'I didn't know you could sing,' Gail said.

'I've not had much cause to over the last few years,' Jess replied.

'Because things were so unhappy at home?' Jess nodded. 'Well, you're out of that now so you can sing as much as you like. We all enjoyed it, especially Carter.' Gail wiggled her eyebrows, making Jess blush. 'Do I detect a little love in the air?'

A huge sigh escaped Jess's lips. 'Would that it was possible, but I'm still married to Bill.'

'So? From what you've said, you're well shot of Bill.'

'I'm terrified Bill will find me and that would cause problems for Carter if… well, you know.'

'Carter knows about your husband so surely it would be up to him whether he wanted to be in a relationship with you,' Gail countered.

'I suppose so. Anyway, I'm not sure Carter is interested.'

'I would argue that point. Jess, life is for living, not just existing. If you have the chance of love, grab it with both hands, because you're a long time dead.'

Jess pondered her friend's words as she drank her tea and couldn't help but think that Gail was absolutely right.

10

Jess shook herself from her own thoughts and instead turned her attention to Gail. 'You know my situation, but what about yours? Tell me all about yourself.'

Gail blew out her cheeks before saying, 'Well, you know I'm twenty-five years old and all I ever wanted to do was be a cook. When my parents died, I got a job in a big house over in the Ladywood area. The trouble was the master there thought I would be more useful in his bedroom than in his kitchen.'

'What did you do?'

'I was cleaning up one evening and he came down to the kitchen. He grabbed me and tried to rape me.'

'Oh my God, Gail! How frightening.'

'I got hold of a knife and waved it in his face and of course he backed off. He was furious that I'd dared to confront him and said he was going to summon the coppers. He told me to get my things and get out.'

'You were very lucky he didn't harm you.'

'I ran upstairs, packed my bag and went back to the kitchen. He'd gone by that time so I trashed the place. Vegetables all over the floor; I emptied flour, sugar, salt, coffee, cocoa – everything I could find all over the kitchen.'

'No!' Jess was aghast.

'Yes! Then I ran. I lived in the park for a while until the park-keeper found me sleeping in his shed. Then I roamed the streets, begging. I lost a lot of weight and then on a cold night one of Ellen's cabbies found me and brought me here. I've been living here ever since.'

'Why do women have to go through so much because of men and their arrogant and abusive behaviour?' Jess said, almost to herself.

'Bastards, most of 'em,' Gail added, taking Jess by surprise.

'Can you imagine a world where women could ever be equal; where we could vote and hold high positions in business?'

'It ain't never gonna happen,' Gail said resignedly. 'Women as doctors or lawyers – even in government? The men would never allow it!'

'Things are beginning to change, though, Gail. Last year a woman called Eliza Orme was the first woman in the United Kingdom to get a law degree. Also this year another called Walkington, I think, graduated with a degree of Bachelor of Laws.'

'How do you know that?' Gail asked, astonished at the statement.

'I read it in the newspaper. As for women in the government, I guess you're right, that won't ever happen, but it's a beautiful dream,' Jess replied with a sigh of longing.

* * *

Over the next days and weeks, Jess noticed Al Flint frequented the bar more and more, often trying his best to get Jess to sing with him again. His efforts were fruitless though; Jess was happy just to serve.

'You should come to the music hall,' he said one day.

'I've been,' Jess answered.

'Ah, but not to see me perform.'

Arrogant bleeder! Carter thought as he hovered close to the pair, not able to resist listening in to their conversation.

'Why not try out for a job there?' the blue-eyed fellow asked.

'But I have a job,' Jess said, spreading her arms to encompass the bar.

'I know but...'

'Do not cast aspersions on my workplace, Mr Flint, or my friends here,' Jess cut across Al firmly.

You tell him, Jess! Carter nodded as he watched the exchange.

'I was about to say that you could earn more money singing on the stage.'

Carter shook his head, thinking, *You're a liar, Flint, that was not what you were about to say at all!*

'Mr Flint, I'm very happy here and have no desire to do anything else,' Jess said.

'If you should change your mind...'

'I won't. Now please excuse me, I believe it's my break time.' Jess left the bar and Carter grinned widely.

'Tough nut to crack, that one,' Flint said.

'She's a lady and I suggest you remember that,' Carter retorted before moving away to serve a waiting customer.

In the kitchen, Jess was telling Ellen, Gail and Kathy what Al had said to her.

'He has a point,' Kathy muttered.

'He's very insistent. I don't think he'll give up that easily,' Jess remarked.

'Would you like me to bar him?' Ellen asked.

Kathy rolled her eyes and sighed.

'No, it's fine. I'll just ignore him. He seems harmless enough,' Jess assured her.

'I'll ask Carter to keep an eye on him,' Ellen said.

'Oh, I think he's doing that already,' Gail said with a cheeky grin, 'because Carter is carrying a candle for our Jess, I think.'

Jess blushed as all eyes turned to her.

'He's a good man, you could do a lot worse,' Ellen said.

'Yes, like that Flint bloke,' Gail added.

No one noticed the look of jealousy on the cleaner's face. Kathy had watched this girl come in and everyone fawn over her. Carter was beside himself for want of her and now this Al was making a move on her too. Kathy's lip curled in disgust as she eyed Jess across the table. *You'll get yours one day, miss, you just wait and see*, she thought with a smirk.

'When you've finished your matchmaking...' Jess said, making Gail and Ellen laugh.

By the time her break was over and she returned to the bar, Jess noticed Al Flint had gone. What she didn't know was that Carter had given the man a stern warning. He had promised Flint a punch on the nose should he continue to harass Jess.

11

Despite being told to leave Jess alone by the barman, Al Flint continued to frequent The Queen's Head during the day. He would have stayed in the evenings too had he not been contracted to sing at the music hall. He was fascinated by the pretty barmaid, and couldn't understand why she preferred serving ale to using her beautiful voice to entertain people. He was certain if she joined the performers, she could be top billing alongside himself.

He noticed on his visits that Jess was keeping very much to herself where he was concerned. He also saw how Carter looked at her and realised the man was in love. *No wonder he warned me off*, he thought.

Al had on occasion tried to coax Jess to sing to the customers again but she was having none of it, so he contented himself with enjoying her beauty and living in hope that she might change her mind.

Hearing shouting, Jess looked up when an argument broke out between two men. 'You'm talking through yer arse!' one shouted.

'I ain't! I'm tellin' yer, I support the best football team in the country!'

Jess shook her head as the two customers bickered but kept an eye on the pair lest a fight ensue. Eventually they agreed to differ and Jess relaxed.

Bella and Enid came in and Jess was glad to see Enid looked completely recovered from her assault, physically at least.

'Give us a couple of gins, darlin',' Bella said, slapping her money on the counter.

Jess obliged before asking, 'How are you feeling, Enid?'

'I'm fine, sweet'eart, thanks for checking.'

'You out tonight?'

'Ar, we 'ave to earn a copper or two,' Bella responded to Jess's question.

'Please be careful.'

'We will. We'm out in pairs now – all the wenches are.'

'How does that work?' Jess asked.

'It means we'm always within sight of each other, and have our whistles handy.'

'I wish you didn't have to go out at all.'

'So do I, lovey, but it's all we know and even if I say so meself – we'm good at it!' Bella's loud laugh carried across the room. They moved to their usual table when another two ladies of the night joined them. Jess hadn't seen the newcomers before; clearly they usually drank elsewhere. She served them with a smile and a kind word before moving on to see to another customer.

'They're new, aren't they?' Ellen's voice said in Jess's ear.

'Yes, maybe all the girls will start coming to The Queen's Head, it would be good for sales if they did.'

'True. Go and have your break and I'll stand in for you,'

Ellen instructed. Then she yelled, 'Right, which of you renegades is next?'

'Me!' called a man.

'No, you ain't! Take yer turn. I'm first and I do love a redhead.'

Ellen laughed and began pouring beer.

In the kitchen, Jess sipped a cup of hot tea, then said, 'We have a couple of unfortunate women in, they're sitting with Bella and Enid.'

'That'll become known as the *Unfortunate Corner*, especially if the rest of them come in,' Gail said. The term was often used for the women patrolling the streets at night; it was a 'nice' way of referring to the prostitutes.

'I'm concerned for them, Gail, what with those murders in Whitechapel.'

'That's London though, it's a long way from here.'

'True, but it only takes a train ride and the murderer could be in Birmingham,' Jess emphasised.

'Worrying won't help because we both know that the girls can't afford to give up their work.'

Over the next half an hour, they discussed the state of the economy, the number of men sent to jail for theft, and how the newspapers sensationalised their columns in order to sell more papers to the gullible public.

'I don't think I'll be reading the papers for a while, it's all too distressing,' Gail said.

Jess nodded and got to her feet. 'Back to the bar for me, see you later.'

Ellen relinquished her role and Jess began to serve once more. From the corner of her eye she would see Al watching her, but she ignored him.

'Gin!' Jess yelled to Carter as Bella approached the counter and a moment later the bottle slid along where she caught it deftly. Pouring the alcohol, she took the money and shouted, 'Coming back!' The bottle whizzed along and she laughed as Carter only just reached it in time.

The two tossed glasses to each other, putting on a show for the drinkers to loud applause. Jess was in her element and loving life.

* * *

Whilst Jess had been building her new life in Birmingham, over in Wednesbury, Jess's friend Peg had been watching Bill Lacey like a hawk. He'd been coming and going at all hours of the day and night and always seemed to have money for booze.

Peg and her husband, Jim, discussed it often and both agreed not to mention it to Jess. If Bill was stealing, then pound to a penny he would be caught eventually. They didn't much care as long as Jess was safe.

It was difficult to find something to say in her letters that didn't involve Bill, but Peg did her best. She included the gossip on the street, Jim's work and how much she was missing her friend. She was glad Jess had finally found some happiness and prayed it would remain so. Not working herself, Peg was also a little envious of Jess's freedom and would have loved a job of her own. Jim, however, had other ideas – *No wife of mine will have to go out to work.*

Peg was not kept short of money, on the contrary she had plenty to go shopping with. It was being home all day on her own that was wearing her down. She had no one to talk to since Jess had left, and only now she began to realise how lonely she was. She decided she would explain how she felt to Jim when he came home, but she suspected she knew what the outcome would be. He would flatly refuse to let her seek a job, but Peg was determined. No matter what he said, she was going to find something to occupy her time other than cooking and cleaning the house.

A good meal should put him in the right mood and then – she would pounce!

Having finished his dinner of fish in parsley sauce with boiled potatoes, Jim sat in his armchair to read the paper.

'Jim, I've made up my mind, I'm gonna look for a job. I'm going mad in this place all by myself day after day.'

Jim sighed, folded the newspaper and laid it in his lap. 'Is this because of Jess?' he asked. Peg frowned. 'Do you want to work because Jess does?'

'No. I've just told you. I'm lonely, Jim, I don't see a soul all day and you're tired when you come home.'

'So you're saying keeping house is not enough for you?'

'Yes. I clean every day so the place is spotless. I need company, Jim, someone to talk to and to do summat apart from dusting, sweeping, washing and cooking.'

'All right, love, if that's what you really want then I'll support you. As you know, I've always been dead set against it, but I do understand that you're lonely, and the extra pennies would come in handy. Just be aware, there's very few jobs on offer out there.'

Peg dropped into her chair, her mouth hanging open with surprise. 'Do you mean it?' she asked, finally locating her tongue.

'I do. What I don't want is for you to get despondent if a job isn't forthcoming.'

'Thank you, sweet'eart. I'll go looking tomorrow.'

Jim nodded and picked up the paper once more.

Peg was overjoyed and as she made a pot of tea she hummed a little tune.

'Peg, love, please don't sing 'cos you sound like a glede under a door.' Jim held up the paper as a shield against the tea towel thrown his way. He chuckled as Peg resumed her singing, louder than ever.

At that moment, Peg had no idea that she would not be searching for work the following day, or for a while after that.

12

That same night after lock-up, Jess and Gail sat in the kitchen chatting and rubbing their feet. They both turned as Carter walked in, saying, 'Jess, I wonder if I might have a word.'

'I was just off to bed anyway,' Gail said with a knowing smile, 'see you both in the morning.'

Carter took the seat Gail had vacated.

'What's on your mind?' Jess asked gently.

'You.'

'Me?'

'Yes. I have to say this before I burst. I can't go on any longer without telling you. Jess, I've fallen in love with you.'

Jess's eyes opened wide in shock. 'I thought... we were just friends. That night after finding Enid, you were a little – aloof.'

'I know and I'm sorry for that. You see, with you not wearing a ring I thought you were single. When you said your injuries were caused by your husband I was devastated.'

'Carter, we can't be together while I'm still wed to Bill, you must know that.'

'I understand, you don't feel the same.' He got to his feet quickly but Jess stopped him.

'Carter, please stay and talk. It's not that I don't feel the same because I do.'

'Oh, Jess!' Carter said, reaching out to her.

'Wait a minute. Sit down and hear me out.' She watched him as he obeyed. 'Now, if you and I were to walk out together, my name would be mud. My reputation would be ruined and you would be called a cad. We would bring shame on ourselves which in turn would reflect badly on Ellen and the others.'

'I agree with what you're saying but I can't help myself, Jess, I'm head over heels for you.'

Tears glinted in Jess's eyes as she replied. 'And I for you, but I don't see a way around it.'

'Only our friends here know you're married, no one else...' Carter began.

'What if Bill finds me? Everyone would know then,' she said sadly.

'Bugger Bill! I can't go on like this, Jess, it's killing me!'

Laying a hand on his arm, she paused. 'If we could be certain...'

'We can! We'll talk to the others and they'll keep our secret. I'd stake my life on it!'

'Maybe you're right. Then let's discuss it with them tomorrow.'

Carter jumped to his feet and asked, 'May I kiss you?'

Jess blushed furiously as she nodded. In a moment she was standing wrapped in Carter's strong arms, his lips on hers. Her blood was on fire as it raged through her veins and she felt light-headed.

Releasing her reluctantly, Carter bid her goodnight and disappeared. Jess slumped into her chair, her head swimming as she placed her fingertips on her mouth. She had never in her life felt so excited, which only proved she too was deeply in love.

* * *

The following morning, when Jess came down to breakfast, she learned Carter had already broached the subject of their discussion. Everyone assured her they would keep closed-mouthed and her secret was safe with them. Jess felt a little embarrassed that Carter had shared their news already, but relieved and happy at their friends' loyalty towards her. All except Kathy, that is. Green with envy, the cleaner stomped from the room.

Later in the day, Al Flint came into The Queen's Head and pushed his way to the counter. 'I have two tickets for the theatre and thought you might like to join me.'

'No, thank you,' Jess replied politely.

'Come on, Jess, a night out will do you good.'

'I can't, Al.'

'Why not?'

'Because I'm promised to another.'

'Ah. Sorry, I didn't know.'

Jess hadn't lied. She was promised to Bill as his wife, but her love was pledged to Carter.

A grin spread across Carter's face as Al sidled away, drink in hand. *That told you, you cocky bugger!* Carter thought. He went about his work feeling much better.

* * *

Whilst Jess had been fending off her admirer, over in Wednesbury her friend Peg was fighting for her life.

Bill Lacey was drunk out of his mind. He had waited for Jim

to leave for work then had banged on Peg's door. As she opened it, Bill pushed his way in.

'Hey!' Peg exclaimed.

'Where is she, Peg?' Bill demanded.

'I've told you, I don't know.'

Bill's arm shot out and he slapped Peg's face so hard her head rocked on her shoulders. 'Where. Is. She?' he asked again.

And again Peg denied knowing Jess's whereabouts. This time Bill's fist caught her squarely on the jaw, knocking her to the floor.

Peg's head reeled and she tried to scramble away but in a flash he was on her. Punching her in the stomach, he knocked the wind out of her. 'Tell me where she is!'

'I don't know,' she gasped. 'Please, Bill...!'

He punched Peg again and again as she desperately tried to get away. She wasn't strong enough to throw him off her so, taking a deep breath, she screamed as loud as she could. Blood poured from her nose and her lips were split. Her eyes began to swell and she was sure he'd cracked a couple of ribs but as yet the pain hadn't registered, adrenaline alone keeping her in the fight.

'Tell me and I'll go,' he said menacingly. Peg's tears ran as she begged him to stop. 'I will as soon as you tell me where Jess is.' With that he hit her again. Now the pain was setting in and her whole body was in agony. Peg crumbled. She knew he would kill her if she didn't admit to knowing where Jess was. She could barely speak but from between bleeding lips she whispered, 'The Queen's Head, Birmingham.'

Bill smacked her once more and walked out, leaving Peg and her blood all over the kitchen floor.

A neighbour, Mr Appleby, had heard the screams and saw Bill leave. Then the elderly man had hobbled to Jim's workplace as fast as he could manage, where he waved his walking stick, calling out for Jim.

'You have to come, Jim! Bill Lacey was in your house and your wife was screaming her head off!'

'Bloody hell! Thanks, Mr Appleby,' Jim said before dropping his tools and racing home where he found his battered wife still lying on the kitchen floor.

'Peg! Oh, my darling, what's he done to you? I'll bloody kill him for this!' he ground out as he gingerly lifted his wife and carried her outside. Whistling for a cab, he yelled, 'Hospital! My wife has been assaulted!'

Peg moaned as the cab moved off and Jim whispered to her. 'It's all right, love, we're going to the hospital. The doctor will give you something for the pain.'

When they arrived, Jim carried Peg indoors after asking the cabbie to wait. A nurse rushed over to him and guided him into a small room. 'A neighbour assaulted her,' Jim explained as he laid his wife on a bed.

'I'll fetch a doctor,' the nurse said and rushed out. A moment later she was back, a silver-haired man in tow.

'Give the nurse your details while I check your wife over.'

Jim did as he was bid whilst Peg was made comfortable.

'What happened, Mr Butler?' the doctor asked once Jim had returned.

'She was assaulted by our drunken neighbour.'

'Do you know why?'

'Because his wife left him after being battered for years, and he wanted to know where she'd gone. Peg and his wife have been friends for a long time.'

'I see. Nurse, get Mrs Butler cleaned up and taken into the ward. I'll prescribe some pain medication. Mr Butler, you may have some time with your wife, but not long. She needs rest.'

'Thank you, doctor.'

A short while later, Jim sat by his wife's bed, holding her hand.

'Jim, I told him. I told Bill where Jess is. He wouldn't stop hitting me!' Peg muttered, her tears running freely. 'It was the only way to stop him.'

'Don't you worry about anything, I'll sort everything out. You need to rest and get better.'

Jim was then ushered out and told to come back at visiting time. He kissed Peg's head and left her in the capable hands of the nurses. The waiting cab took him home and once there he paid the fare and went indoors. From the cabinet in the living room he pulled out a bottle of whisky and marched out of the house. Banging on Mr Appleby's door, he presented the elderly man with the bottle by way of thanks. He had very different plans for his other neighbour.

13

'How is Mrs Butler?'

'Not good.'

'I couldn't get to you any quicker on these old legs,' the old man apologised.

'I appreciate that you came at all, but you should have sent a runner.'

Mr Appleby chuckled. 'I never thought of that, I was just in shock.'

'It was good of you, Mr Appleby. Peg's in the hospital, she'll be all right but it will take time.'

'I'm only sorry I couldn't help her,' the old fellow lamented.

'Then you'd be in a bed next to Peg. You did the right thing, Mr Appleby. Now, are you sure it was Bill Lacey you saw come out of our house?'

'Yes, lad. He was blind drunk, weaving all over the place and rubbing his hand.'

Jim winced. 'Peg said it was him too. There was a bit of me that was hoping she was mistaken.'

'What will you do?'

'I'm going back to work now, but I'll be having words with Mr Lacey soon enough, you can be sure of that.'

'Be careful, lad. Find a gin pit to have those words over,' Mr Appleby said with a wink.

Jim thought about the deep pits left behind by those mining for coal. They were death traps if you didn't know where they were, and many unfortunates had gone missing trying to traverse the heath over the years.

After saying his last thanks, Jim went home and cleaned the kitchen floor, fuming at the sight of his wife's blood. Then he returned to work, his mates crowding around him as he explained what had happened. The boss was there too and Jim smiled when he said, 'This job can wait a while. You lot get off and help Jim find and sort this bloke out. I'll see you back here tomorrow.'

Without a second's hesitation, the men laid down their tools and walked off the site and Jim and three of his friends went back to his house to formulate a plan.

* * *

Immediately after he had left Peg's house, Bill Lacey had weaved his way to the railway station. He bought a ticket to Birmingham and staggered onto the platform. Pulling a half bottle of gin from his pocket, he took a swig before replacing it. 'Watcha lookin' at?' he asked aggressively.

The two women he aimed his question at turned away and walked further along the platform, disgust all over their faces.

Bill muttered to himself as he shuffled his feet, trying to keep his balance.

'Now then, Bill, we're not gonna have any trouble from you, are we?' a voice asked.

'No, Tom, me old mate, I'm going to Brum to fetch me wife home,' Bill said, slapping the porter on the back. With a nod, the man moved away. Bill grinned before he pulled out the bottle once more and finished the gin. From habit he pushed the empty bottle back into his jacket pocket.

The huff of the train sounded as it slowed to a halt and immediately passengers scrambled to board. Bill was jostled as he fought his way to the third-class carriage. Pushing women aside, he found a seat on the wooden boards where he leaned his head back and closed his eyes. It wouldn't be long now until he found Jess and when he did she would rue the day she had left him.

Bill's loud snores made the people around him shake their heads, and even the jerk of the engine setting off didn't wake him. Children howled with laughter when Bill farted in his sleep, their mothers grumbling in disgust at the drunken man.

Bill woke with a start as he felt himself being shaken. 'End of the line, pal,' a porter said. Nodding, Bill got to his feet unsteadily and staggered to the door. 'Get out of the way!' he yelled as people tried to board. Taking a step down, he missed his footing and fell heavily onto the concrete platform. With a titter, he raised himself up and weaved his way through the crowds to the exit. Here he glanced around, blinking in the bright sunshine. 'Right, Jess, I'm coming for you so you'd best be ready.' With that, Bill Lacey picked his way along the street towards the market.

* * *

Back at Brick Kiln Croft, Jim and his friends agreed a plan. Firstly they went to Bill's house and banged on the door. Jim peered through the window but could see no one. Going around the back, he looked into the kitchen, again the room was empty. Bill was not at home.

They decided Bill must have gone to the railway station to catch a train, and late in the afternoon they too set off for the station. They realised that they would most likely have missed the train Bill had caught, but could catch the next one. Then they would race to The Queen's Head. Once there they would coax Bill out of the pub and find a nice quiet spot where they could explain to him the error of his ways.

Boarding the train in Wednesbury, Jim and his pals sat quietly. A whistle blew and carriage doors were slammed shut, then the engine chugged and clouds of steam raced past the window as the train moved forward.

'We'll get him,' one of Jim's friends said.

Jim nodded. 'Ar, Harry, we will.'

Nothing further was said on the journey, each man eager to help their friend avenge poor Peg.

14

Bill meandered along the street, still worse for wear from the gin he'd drunk earlier. Despite asking for directions, he couldn't remember what he'd been told, even though it was only a moment ago. Seeing a pub, he decided to pop in and have a couple of beers which he was sure would help clear his head. After all, he was in no hurry now he knew where his wife was. Leaving the public house, Bill meandered his way along the street, trying to dodge people walking in the opposite direction. It wasn't long before he came across another pub and he grinned. 'I'll just have another snifter before I go to...' He scratched his head, trying to recall why he was here. Looking around, he didn't recognise where *here* was so with a shrug of his shoulders he pushed open the door and went inside. Having consumed more gin, Bill suddenly remembered why he'd come to Birmingham and he pushed his way roughly through the crowd to leave the bar. Anger flowed through him like a fire as he staggered his way along the street, all the while muttering to himself. 'I'm coming for you, Jess. Ain't you gonna be surprised when you see me? I'll tell you summat else an' all, you won't ever think of leaving me again by the time I'm finished with you!'

* * *

In the meantime, Jim's train had arrived at New Street station and he and his mates rushed outside. They hailed a cab and Jim asked to be taken to The Queen's Head. 'I hope we're in time,' Jim mumbled as the cab set off.

'Either way, we'll find him, Jim, don't worry about that,' Bert said.

'Ar and when we do...' George added, raising a fist.

'We stick to the plan. Get Bill drunk as a lord and home, then we can sort him out,' Jim insisted.

No sooner had the cab stopped than the men piled out. Jim paid the cabbie and then said, 'Remember, no violence in here.' Then he led his friends indoors.

Glancing around, they saw no sign of Bill and exchanged puzzled looks. Going to the bar, Jim called out, 'Jess.'

'Jim! What are you doing here?' Jess asked as she turned and saw her old neighbour, suddenly feeling very afraid. Carter moved to her side and Jess said, 'Carter, this is Jim, husband to my friend, Peg.' Carter nodded a greeting.

'Jess, Bill knows where you are! Has he been here?' Jim's words came out in a panicked rush.

'No. Oh, God!' Jess's face drained of colour and her knees gave way. Carter caught her and steadied her.

'Peg's in the hospital, Jess, he beat her senseless!' Jim said angrily.

'Oh, no! Jim, I'm so sorry. I have to go to her.'

'No! You must get out of sight. He's bound to be on the way here. We'll wait for him,' Jim said.

'Come on, Jess, stay in the kitchen until all this is over,' Carter said, pushing her out of the bar. Explaining to Gail what was going on, Carter returned to his place behind the counter.

Jim ordered beers for him and his three friends and then all they could do was wait. Nobody saw Kathy, the cleaner, slip out through the door. Out on the pavement she too waited – for a drunk named Bill. This was the chance she'd been hoping for, an opportunity to finally get rid of Jess Lacey. Once that was achieved, maybe then Carter would notice her. Kathy was sure they could become a couple if Jess was out of the picture. She could make Carter happier than Jess ever could.

At the corner of the building, Kathy watched people passing by. She had no idea what this Bill looked like but guessed he'd be doing a drunken dance up the street. All she had to do then was ask his name. Once she was certain she had the right man, then she could put her plan into action. If it worked then Kathy Frith was set to become a wealthy woman.

It was the sound of his singing which caught her attention and Kathy smiled. She watched the man stop and look up at the pub sign. As he made to enter, she called to him. 'Are you Bill Lacey?'

Blinking rapidly, Bill turned to the woman addressing him and nodded. 'What of it?'

'I have some information for you, but it will cost you,' Kathy said as she crooked a finger.

Bill sidled over to her. 'What infimation?' He tittered at his mispronunciation.

'Money first. Ten bob.'

'Ten shillings! Are you mad, woman? I ain't never seen that much money!' Bill laughed and turned away.

'Wait! Two bob.' Kathy was getting desperate.

'Look, lady, I don't know what your game is but...'

'I know where your wife is,' Kathy whispered.

'So do I, now bugger off!'

'I know summat else an' all,' Kathy said tantalisingly.

Bill pushed his head forward, trying to focus on the woman before him. 'What?'

'Two bob,' Kathy insisted.

Bill dug in his pocket and pulled out a sixpence. 'A tanner,' he said, offering her the coin.

Kathy snatched it, saying, 'There's four blokes in there waiting for you.'

'Why?' Bill asked.

'To buy you a drink, why do you think?' Kathy rolled her eyes then disappeared around the back of the building.

Her sarcasm was completely lost on Bill as he mumbled, 'That's nice of them.' Pushing the pub door open, he stepped inside and shoved his way to the bar.

15

'He's here,' Harry said quietly.

'If you need some help...' Carter offered as he glared at the inebriated man pushing through the crowd.

'We'll be fine, mate, but thanks for the offer,' Jim said.

'Jim! I d'aint expect to see you here,' Bill said, recognising his neighbour.

'How do, Bill. Me and the lads are out for a good time.'

Bill nodded to Jim's friends. It never occurred to him that Jim might have already found his injured wife and be gunning for him.

'Join us for a drink?' Jim asked.

'I don't mind if I do,' Bill responded, having completely forgotten why he was there.

'Whisky for my friend, please, bar-keeper,' Jim called out.

Carter obliged, keeping an eye on the little group.

In the kitchen, Jess was sitting stock still, almost afraid to breathe. Gail made yet more tea and Ellen talked quietly, reassuring Jess that everything would be fine.

Suddenly Jess got to her feet and prowled the kitchen like a caged animal. 'He mustn't find me,' she whispered. 'If he does, he'll kill me!'

'You're safe here with us,' Ellen said.

'He knows I'm here, Ellen! I'm putting everyone in danger.'

'You should have thought of that before,' Kathy muttered under her breath.

'No, love. He only thinks you're here, he doesn't know for sure because he hasn't seen you.'

Jess held her head in her hands for a moment before she continued her pacing. 'He'll keep coming back until he finds me. I have to get away!'

'It would be best,' Kathy put in, only to receive a scowl from Ellen.

'Jess, stop it!' Gail's words were quiet but stern. 'Sit down and think about what Ellen is telling you.'

Nodding, Jess dropped onto a chair and listened to Ellen. 'We won't let him anywhere near you even if he does see you. I'll hire a bodyguard if needs be.'

Gail folded her arms around her friend as Jess dissolved into tears.

'Won't do no good,' Kathy mumbled as she sat at the table, her hand in her pocket clutching the sixpence tightly. It wasn't what she'd hoped for but it was a tanner more than she'd had yesterday. She waited with bated breath to hear the fighting start in the bar, but when it didn't she began to wonder what was happening.

Instead of throwing punches, the men were laughing and drinking and eventually Carter called time.

'Come on, Bill, let's have summat to eat then we can carry on drinking,' Jim said as Bert and Harry helped Bill sway his way out of the pub. To Carter, Jim whispered, 'Tell Jess to fear no more. Nobody will ever find the body.' With a wink, Jim followed his friends.

Carter locked up, hardly able to believe what he'd been told. Was the man being serious or was his statement a sick joke? Should he tell Jess what Jim had said or say nothing? It would worry Jess if she knew but he couldn't bear to see her living in constant fear of her husband returning.

Going to the kitchen, Carter blurted out everything, including Jim's final ominous words.

'That's it then,' Jess said resignedly.

'What, love?' Gail asked.

'By the morning Bill will be dead!'

'No, I'm sure that won't be the case,' Ellen said.

'Bill battered Jim's wife and put her in the hospital. There is no way Jim will allow that to go unpunished, Ellen. He adores his wife and now Bill will suffer the same fate or worse.'

'Don't feel sorry for him, Jess, not after what he's done,' Gail urged.

'I don't, Gail,' Jess replied.

'Then what is it?' Carter asked.

'Don't you see? If Bill is dead and not found I will never be free of him. I won't be able to prove he's dead without implicating Jim, and I can't divorce a missing man.' Suddenly overwhelmed by it all, Jess burst into tears.

In an instant, Carter wrapped her in his arms, kissing her hair.

Kathy watched, her lips drawn into a tight line. If Jess couldn't get a divorce, then she couldn't wed Carter. Slowly a smile formed on her face – there was still a chance for her with Carter after all.

'None of that matters now, the most important thing is to

keep you safe,' Carter said. 'We'll know more tomorrow, I'm sure.'

* * *

Out in the street, Bill was being held up by Harry and Bert as they walked him out of the pub.

'Jess is in there, you know,' Bill said suddenly, recalling why he was in Birmingham.

'She ain't, pal,' Jim said. 'It's my guess she's at home waiting for you.'

'Nah, she's been gone too long to come back just like that.' Bill tried to snap his fingers but couldn't manage it.

Jim hailed a cab and called out an address while the others bundled Bill inside.

'It'll cost you extra if he chucks up in my cab,' Ernie, Ellen's brother and the cab driver, said. Ernie's cab was waiting right outside his sister's pub where he parked up every night waiting for a fare.

'He won't, he'll be asleep in a minute,' Jim assured the man.

Sure enough, before the cab reached the end of the road, Bill Lacey was snoring loudly.

16

Having travelled from Birmingham to Wednesbury, the cab rolled to a stop in the middle of a moonless night, and the cabbie looked around as the men spilled from the carriage. 'Are you sure this is the right place, fella? There's nowt here but a building site.'

Jim walked to where the cabbie sat. 'That drunk assaulted two women, one of whom was my wife. He beat her so badly she's in the hospital. Now let me ask you a question. If you were me – what would you do about it?'

Ernie recalled the pretty young woman he had brought to his sister, Ellen, some time ago, her face a mass of bruises. Could she have been one of the women the drunk had beaten or was it just a coincidence? Drawing in a breath, he said, 'I'd do the same to him.'

Jim nodded and handed up the fare as well as a large tip. 'You don't know a thing.'

'I ain't been out of Brum all night, mate. Just make a good job of it.' With that the cabbie flicked the reins and the cab disappeared into the darkness.

Bill was groaning as he was carried into the shell of a newly constructed building.

'George, keep watch,' Jim said as he followed the others. The site was well away from other dwellings so he was not concerned that they would be seen or heard.

'Okay, but I'm not sure this is such a good idea bringing him here. It's our workplace, Jim! Maybe we should take him out on the heath,' George said.

'We'll be all right, just keep an eye out,' Jim replied.

Dumping Bill on the ground, Harry and Bert stepped back.

'Bill!' Jim slapped the man around the face to wake him up.

'What? Stop it!' Bill pushed Jim's hand away.

'Do you remember what you did to my Peg?'

'Look, Jimbo...' Bill's head shot back as the punch landed on his chin. 'Ow! Bloody hell, that hurt,' he moaned, rubbing the sore area.

'You beat up my wife, Bill, and that's something I cannot forgive!' Jim's face was close to Bill's and he could smell the stale alcohol.

'I just gave her a little tap so she'd tell me where Jess was.'

'A little tap! You almost killed her, you bastard!' Jim's leg shot out and he heard a satisfying crunch as his boot snapped one of Bill's ribs.

Bill howled and rolled himself into a ball.

'Keep him quiet, noise carries further at night!' George said from the front of the building.

Bert whipped a handkerchief from his pocket and stuffed it into Bill's mouth.

'Argh!' Bill tried to remove the gag but Bert and Harry held his arms.

Jim rolled up his shirt sleeves, saying, 'Now you're gonna know how my Peg felt when you battered her senseless.' Jim lashed out with his fists using every ounce of energy he could muster. He kicked and punched until he was utterly spent. Breathing hard, he dropped to the ground, looking at the bloody mess that was once his neighbour.

Bert leaned over Bill and checked for a pulse. Shaking his head, he said, 'He's done for.'

'What shall we do with the body?' Harry asked. 'We'll need to find a deep gin pit.'

Jim thought for a moment then said, 'Change of plan. Leave him there.'

'What about the coppers?' George asked as he joined the others.

'The gaffer will find him in the morning and fetch the bobbies to investigate. Of course we don't know a thing,' Jim explained, rubbing his aching hands.

'We could bury him in the concrete, no one would ever find him,' Bert suggested.

'No, Jess and Peg need to know he's dead and can never hurt them again. There are no witnesses other than the cabbie, whose word I trust, so we're free and clear. Come on, let's go home.' Jim was helped to his feet and the four friends strode away from the murder scene without a backward glance.

* * *

The following morning, Jim boarded the first train back to Birmingham, then took a cab to The Queen's Head. He asked the cabbie to wait then hammered on the door to the pub until it was opened by Carter.

'Come in,' Carter urged before re-locking the door.

Jim was led into the kitchen where Jess was sitting with the others.

'Jim!' Jess gasped.

'Bill is gone, Jess, he won't ever hurt you again.'

Jess drew in a breath, her hand over her mouth. 'Gone?'

'He's dead, love. We left him on our building site. I expect the gaffer has found him by now and summoned the constabulary. I'm sorry, Jess, but I warned him countless times about hitting you, but when he set about Peg – well, it was a step too far.' Jim glanced around at the shocked faces and only then did he begin to worry about whether all present would keep their secret, but there was nothing to be done about that now. He had murdered Bill Lacey and his friends were accomplices so all he could do was to pray everyone here would keep their mouths tightly shut.

'Oh, Jim, what if the police discover what you've done?' Jess asked once her shock had started to dissipate.

'They won't. There were no witnesses, we made sure of that,' Jim replied.

Is that so? Kathy thought as she listened to the conversation. *We've just heard you admit to killing a man.*

'Only we know and no one here will say a word,' Ellen put in as she glanced around at each face.

'I'd best get back. I expect the police will be in touch with you at some point to let you know of his demise.'

Jess threw her arms around Jim. 'Be careful.'

'Once the coppers have been to see you, maybe you could visit Peg, I know she'd love to see you.'

'I will, Jim, and – thank you.'

Jim was shown out by Carter and when he returned the kitchen was abuzz with conversation. The only one not participating was Kathy. She was plotting the next step in her plan to be rid of Jess Lacey.

17

The building site was at a standstill when Jim finally arrived for work.

'Where the bloody hell have you been?' the boss yelled.

'I was late getting up. I had a skinful last night, sorry. What's going on?'

'We found a body this morning and now we've got the coppers all over the place!' the gaffer said loudly, then more quietly added, 'Couldn't you have left him somewhere else?'

Jim gave an apologetic shrug of his shoulders, then said, 'Bloody hell!' as he followed his employer to the scene of the crime.

'We don't know who it is,' the boss said.

'Step back, please, sir,' a constable said, using his arm as a barrier.

'Jesus! Officer, I know that man – he's my neighbour!' Jim exclaimed.

'Come with me,' the young policeman said, leading Jim to an older man. 'Sergeant, this man says he knows the deceased.'

'Thanks, I'll deal with it. Go and keep those workers away while we wait for the meat wagon.'

'Yes, sir.' The bobby walked away.

'The meat wagon?' Jim asked.

'My apologies, I'm afraid that was not very professional of me. The coroner's carriage is what I meant. Now, sir, if I can take some details from you.' The sergeant pulled out a small notebook and a nub of a pencil.

Jim could feel the eyes of his friends on him but managed to ignore them.

Licking the lead of the pencil, the sergeant asked, 'Name?'

'Jim Butler.'

'His name,' the exasperated sergeant said, pointing his pencil in the direction of the body.

'Bill Lacey.'

'Address?'

'Mine or his?' Jim asked.

'Yours.'

'Twenty-two Brick Kiln Croft. Bill lives – lived – at number twenty-four.'

'Any idea who may have done this?'

'Bill was not well liked, sergeant. He was a drunk and a bully. His wife, Jess, left him after years of suffering his violence.' Jim watched the man take notes. 'He put my wife in the hospital trying to find out where Jess went.'

'Did he now? And how did you feel about that?' the sergeant asked, suddenly aware of the big man he was speaking to.

'I was angry, of course, but Peg begged me to leave it alone. She was afraid I might get hurt.'

The policeman rolled his eyes over Jim's muscular body before raising an eyebrow and saying, 'Really? Where were you last evening, Mr Butler?'

'Me and the lads went on the lash, that's why I was late to work this morning.' All the time they had been talking, Jim kept his hands in his trouser pockets to hide the bruises just beginning to show.

'Do you know where I can find the deceased's wife?'

'Yes sir. She's at The Queen's Head in Birmingham. She wrote to my wife once she was settled.'

'I think that's everything for now. Thank you, Mr Butler.'

'Poor old Bill, somebody made a real mess of him,' Jim said, shaking his head.

'Indeed,' the sergeant agreed before walking away.

Jim joined his friends, a little frown warning them not to say a word.

Before long, the coroner's wagon arrived and Bill's broken body was lifted inside. The police interviewed all the workers on site before leaving to head back to the station.

Jim and his pals heaved a sigh of relief before work finally began for the day in earnest. 'What do you reckon?' Bert asked as he helped Jim lay some bricks.

'We're fine, there's no evidence to lead the coppers to us. Stop fretting.'

At the end of the day, Jim went home, washed and changed his clothes and set off for the hospital. Stepping through the double doors, he walked along the corridor. The green-painted walls gave the place a drab effect and the smell of sickness made him wrinkle his nose. The ward was brighter, with natural light flooding through the large windows. He hurried to his wife, who was in the last bed in the row.

'Hello, sweetheart, how are you feeling?'

'I'm all right, I just want to go home,' Peg croaked. Her face was swollen and her eyes were turning black from the punches inflicted on her. She groaned as she tried to sit up, holding her ribs.

Jim plumped her pillows and helped make her more comfortable. 'A few more days and you can. We need to make sure you are well enough,' he said, planting a kiss on her forehead.

'I'm scared, Jim... what if Bill is waiting...?'

Jim leaned in close and whispered, 'Bill is gone, love.'

'Gone where?'

'The police found his body this morning.' Jim rubbed his knuckles in a silent message to his wife, telling her what he'd been up to.

'Oh, Jim! Do they know what happened?'

'Just that he was beaten to death. Jess knows and she'll come and see you when she can.'

Peg tried to smile at that but winced at the pain in her jaw. 'Thank you, darlin'.'

'Nobody hurts my girl and gets away with it. All you have to do now is to get well.'

The two held hands and chatted quietly until the hand bell sounded, denoting the end of visiting time.

'I'll see you tomorrow, sweetheart,' Jim said, giving Peg a gentle kiss.

Peg watched her man stride from the ward and she sighed. She felt so lucky to have him as her husband; they were still so much in love even after ten years of marriage. He doted on her, despite her being unable to give him children, saying he was happy as they were. Now he had killed for her and the thought made her shudder.

A nurse rushed over, saying, 'Are you cold? I can close the window.'

'No, I'm fine, thank you,' Peg replied.

Oh, Nurse Karen, if only you knew what gave me the shivers, she thought as she closed her eyes, suddenly feeling tired to the bone.

18

The sun was beating down strong and hot when the Wednesbury police came knocking on the door of The Queen's Head public house.

'Good morning, sir,' the sergeant said to Carter when he opened the door. 'I'd like to speak with Mrs Lacey.'

'Come in,' Carter said. He re-locked the door and led the sergeant and constable through to the kitchen. 'Jess, the police are here to see you.'

'Me?' Jess asked, acting surprised. Jim had warned her they would come and to be on her guard.

'Mrs Lacey?'

'Yes. What's this about, sergeant?'

'I wonder if we could have a moment of privacy.'

'Whatever it is,' Jess said, 'it can be said in front of my friends.'

With a nod, the sergeant went on. 'I'm afraid I have to tell you that we found your husband's body two days ago.'

Jess dropped onto a chair, feigning shock. 'What happened?'

'Someone beat him to death.'

'Oh, good grief!' Jess's hand covered her mouth.

Kathy watched the drama play out, thinking, *You're good, Jess Lacey, I have to hand it to you.*

'I have some questions if you're up to it,' the sergeant added. At her nod, he asked, 'I believe you left him because of his violence towards you?'

'Yes, I couldn't take any more so I ran away.'

'Did you know your husband beat your neighbour's wife and put her in the hospital?'

'Oh, no! Is she all right?' Jess jumped to her feet.

'She's recovering nicely. It appears Mr Lacey was under the impression Mrs Butler knew your whereabouts.'

'Yes, I wrote to Peg once I was settled here. Oh, I wish I hadn't now!'

'It's my thinking it wouldn't have made much difference. Mrs Lacey, have you seen your husband since you left?'

'No, sergeant, I haven't,' Jess answered truthfully.

No, but I have, Kathy thought.

'Do you know anything that could help us with our enquiries?'

Jess shook her head but said nothing.

Clever, Kathy thought, *not committing yourself, Jess.*

'Very well, thank you for your time. I know where you are should there be more questions.'

Carter saw the policemen out and Jess blew out her cheeks with relief.

'Well done, Jess,' Ellen said.

'Do you realise we're all accessories to murder?' Jess asked. 'We could all go to jail for what we know and not telling the police.'

'Would you rather see Jim in jail or dancing on the end of a rope?' Gail asked.

'Of course not...'

'Well then. It seems to me that Jim has done us all a favour by getting rid of that rat!'

Jess looked around at the nodding heads – all except Kathy, who lowered her eyes.

'Thank you, everyone, I'm sorry to have brought this upon you,' Jess said.

'It's done now so worry no more. In fact, I suggest you take the day off and go and see your friend in the hospital,' Ellen urged.

'Thanks, Ellen. I'd love to see Peg if you really can spare me.' Jess went to her room to change, feeling excited at seeing Peg again. Saying she would be back later, Jess left the pub with a spring in her step. She felt light and happy, knowing she was safe at last. Hailing a cab to New Street station, Jess settled for the short ride. After buying a return ticket at the kiosk, she walked onto the platform. The rail tracks criss-crossed beneath the foot bridge before following their path to the next town. Jess moved out of the sun to stand beneath the huge shelter which was held up by sturdy concrete supports. The smell of sooty steam hung in the air, despite there not being a train in the station. Jess glanced up and down the track, willing the engine to come into view. Ten minutes later she was sitting in the third-class carriage, impatient to be on the move.

The whistle blew and the train began to chug as it lurched forward. Picking up speed, the clackety-clack of the iron wheels on the track had a somniferous effect, making Jess feel a little drowsy. The journey of eight miles passed quickly and Jess got to her feet before the train had completely stopped. She staggered as the engine came to a halt with a jolt then made her way to the door. Porters along the platform began to open the doors and help people down. Jess gave one such man a smile with her thanks and alighting, she walked briskly out of the station. Looking around for a cab, she spotted a flower seller sitting on a low wall nearby. She bought some yellow roses then waved to a cabbie.

'Moxley isolation hospital, please,' Jess called out.

'Very good, miss,' the cabbie replied.

Climbing aboard, Jess was on the last leg of her journey. She thought about the place her friend was recovering in; built to house people suffering from diseases such as scarlet fever, diphtheria and typhoid, it also administered to those such as Peg. With luck, her friend would be sent home very soon.

Paying the cabbie, Jess went in through the double doors and walked along the corridor. The top half of the walls were painted cream, the lower half in pale green which did nothing to make one feel comfortable or welcome. There was a sharp smell of disinfectant, causing Jess to wrinkle her nose. Her boots tapped on the linoleum flooring as she stepped forward, wondering which of the many doors she should take. Seeing a nurse, she asked where Peg Butler was.

'It's not visiting time until two o'clock,' the nurse informed her.

'I've come from Birmingham to see her, having taken time off work,' Jess pleaded.

'Ask the sister through there.' The nurse pointed to an office door.

Giving her thanks, Jess tapped lightly on the door.

'Come in.'

Opening the door, Jess peeped inside. 'I'm sorry to disturb you but the nurse said to ask you if I might visit my friend, Mrs Butler.'

'It's not...' the sister began.

'I know, the nurse said two o'clock, but I've taken time off from my job in Birmingham and have to be back this afternoon.'

'It's highly irregular... but I think your visit could well help Mrs Butler recover quicker. So, I will allow you one hour.'

'Thank you, Sister.' Jess entered the ward and spotted Peg instantly. Rushing forward, she gasped at her friend's injuries. Peg's eyes were turning black and were swollen, she had a cut above one eyebrow. Her lip was twice its normal size, showing signs of having been split quite badly. She appeared to be bruised from her head down and Jess wondered how she had survived the vicious attack.

'Jess!'

'Hello, you.' Jess very gently hugged Peg and laid the flowers on the bedside cabinet. 'Oh, Peg, I'm so sorry!'

'All's well now, so don't be.' Peg tried to wink but couldn't quite manage it, causing Jess to laugh.

In her office, the sister smiled. Clearly she'd done the right thing allowing the visit. About twenty minutes later she smiled again at the laughter coming from the whole ward. Whatever the visitor was saying, it was a tonic to her patients, in which case, she decided, the girl could stay as long as she wanted to.

19

Whilst Jess and Peg were enjoying their visit together, and Jess was telling everyone about her antics at the pub, a discussion was underway in Birmingham.

'We must keep tight-lipped about everything,' Ellen said.

'It's vital if we are to keep Jess, and ourselves, safe,' Gail added.

Kathy said nothing, she just sat with the usual scowl on her face.

'At least Jess and I can walk out together now,' Carter put in.

'Don't be too overt about it though because it's early days yet, and we don't want the constabulary sniffing around again.' Carter nodded in agreement at Ellen's warning.

'I wonder if Jess will arrange the funeral,' Gail mumbled.

'I wouldn't if it was me. Let the parish pay for it,' Carter said. 'I doubt Jess could afford it anyway.'

'She has her wages,' Kathy said without thinking.

'Funerals are expensive,' Ellen advised, 'so I agree with Carter. The parish will cover it. Now I suggest we open up before the punters break the door down.'

Carter unlocked the pub door and took his place behind the bar.

Bella and Enid were first in. 'What were the coppers after?' Bella asked before even ordering her usual gin.

Carter explained as he poured the alcohol. 'Jess's husband was found dead.'

'Blimey! Poor wench,' Enid said.

'Not really, Jess was hiding from him because he beat her badly and often,' Carter said.

'Oh, well, in that case, good riddance to bad rubbish!'

All three shared a laugh at Enid's words as more people flooded into the bar room.

'Good day to you.' Carter nodded to Al, the music hall singer. 'Jess not working today?'

'No.'

Ordering a pint of porter, Al surveyed the room. It had been a while since he was last here and he'd been looking forward to seeing Jess. He was sorely disappointed that she wasn't there. 'When will Jess be back?'

'No idea.' Carter's sharp answer warned Al to ask no more questions.

Bella and Enid watched the exchange and grinned. 'That fella had better watch his step,' Bella said.

'Ar, 'cos Carter will have him measure his length on the floor in no time,' Enid agreed. They watched Al move amongst the crowd chatting here and there with the customers. He laughed and joked with some as he sipped his beer, but always his eyes were drawn back to the bar in the hope of seeing Jess return. Then they saw him drink up, place his empty glass on a nearby table and leave.

'There'll be trouble there, you mark my words,' Bella said.

'I hope so, I love a good punch-up,' Enid replied. 'Another gin?'

Bella nodded.

Carter served Enid then went to collect empty glasses. Working the bar was no fun without Jess, and he waited eagerly for her return.

* * *

Upstairs, Kathy was dusting the bedrooms and thinking hard. She could tell the police what she knew about the murder, but would she be given jail time for withholding information? Besides, it wouldn't implicate Jess unless she said Jess and Jim were in it together. She dismissed the idea, realising it carried no weight.

Her mind shifted to her meeting with Bill Lacey. Sitting on the end of Ellen's bed, she pulled out the sixpence he had given her in exchange for information. Looking at the coin, she grinned as the germ of a notion took root. Replacing the coin in her pocket, she got to her feet, dancing around the room and flicking her duster here, there and everywhere. Now she had a much better plan and if she played it right, it would be a gift that would keep on giving.

* * *

Over in Wednesbury, Jess hugged her friend gently and waved goodbye to her fellow patients. Tapping the sister's door, she popped her head around it. 'Thank you so much for letting me visit Peg. I'm sorry if I've overstayed.'

'That's all right. Hearing my patients laughing was a joy. It does them far more good than any medicine. Do come again.'

'Thank you.' Jess smiled and closed the door. Then she left to go back to her work in Birmingham.

The summer set in, the sun burning any skin exposed to it and everyone complained of the heat. Doors were propped open front and back, allowing any breeze to waft through and cool the rooms. Women fanned their faces constantly and men stripped to the waist whilst going about their work. Even the children found shade to sit and play marbles.

Jess was visited and informed by the sergeant that her husband had been buried in a pauper's grave.

'There's no new evidence or leads relating to the manner of his death, so I'm afraid we're closing the case,' he told her.

Once the sergeant had left, Jess finally relaxed. She felt free at last and Jim was safe. A letter arrived later that day from Peg saying she was home and healing well so Jess decided to write back, saying she would visit when she could get time off work.

Life in the pub slowly returned to normal with Jess and Carter entertaining the customers, the only fly in the ointment being Al Flint. He went to the bar every day and tried his best to engage Jess in conversation. Jess, for her part, did what she could to ignore him. Carter kept a close eye on the man but he could feel his patience running out.

Bella and Enid watched with anticipation, knowing the situation would come to a head sooner or later. And so it did.

One exceptionally hot day, Al was pestering Jess as was his wont and Jess finally snapped.

'Look, I've told you countless times I don't have time to chat with you. This is my work and I'm busy, so please leave me alone.' Jess glared at the man who was making her feel incredibly uncomfortable.

'Jess, I don't mean to upset you...'

'Well, you are! If you persist I will have you barred.'

'Ooh, it's warming up now,' Enid said, rubbing her hands together.

'You're a bloodthirsty madam, Enid, and no mistake!' Bella said, shaking her head.

Enid tittered then replied, 'I'm just waiting for Carter to step in.'

Bella went to order more gin, saying loudly, 'Some people don't know when to give up and go home.'

'I beg your pardon?' Flint asked.

Bella turned to face the man, her thick make-up harsh in the light from the windows. 'Jess ain't interested, mate, so why don't you take the hint?'

'Firstly, I'm not your mate, and secondly, it's none of your business!'

Bella drew herself up to her full height, towering over him and looking more like a man than a woman. 'That's my friend you are harassing so it is my business. Now, if you wish to take this outside – I'm ready.'

A hush fell over the room as all ears turned to the pair.

'I'm not going to fight a woman!'

Disappointed groans sounded low before silence resumed.

'Coward,' Bella mumbled.

'Look here! I've come to have a quiet drink...'

'No, you ain't! You've come 'ere to pester Jess and she's fed up to the back teeth with it!' Bella yelled.

Ellen and Gail came through to see what the commotion was, and Carter held out an arm to keep them back. Kathy eyed the scene from her seat by the bar.

'Then let Jess tell me that,' Flint said cockily. He glanced around at the faces watching the contretemps, feeling everyone was on his side.

'She's told you often enough, pal, so take the hint and sling your hook!' Bella growled.

'Look, lady, sit yourself down and shut yer gob!' The moment the words left his lips, Al knew he'd made a mistake. The look on Bella's face told him he'd taken one step too far.

'Oh, bugger it, I've had enough of this.' Bella formed a fist, drew back her arm and planted a punch squarely on Al Flint's chin. An audible intake of breath from the punters preceded groans as men rubbed their own faces, imagining the pain caused by the large fist.

Out for the count before he hit the deck, Flint folded at the knees and slid to the floor.

Applause and cheers filled the room and Bella took a bow.

20

Once Flint came round, he was escorted from the premises by a couple of the customers.

Jess and Carter exchanged a warm smile and Bella was treated to a free gin, much to her delight.

Sidling up to Jess, Carter said, 'You and I should go out to dinner one evening.'

'I'd like that but who would tend the bar?'

'Ellen and maybe Gail could help out.'

'Well, we could ask,' Jess said, feeling excited at the prospect of finally being able to walk out with Carter.

They broached the subject later when the pub had been locked up for the night.

'Yes, of course,' Ellen said, 'but could you make it in the week when we're not so busy?' It was agreed for Wednesday, two days hence.

The only one not happy about it was Kathy. Slipping out of the kitchen unnoticed, she went to her room, where she paced the floor. Emotions flooded through her; hurt that Carter had asked Jess out instead of her, and anger that Jess had accepted.

Why did Kathy seem to be invisible to Carter? It was as if he didn't know she existed. They used to chat when she cleaned the bar and he was restocking, but since the arrival of Jess there was nothing, no flicker of attention or friendship.

Kathy seethed at Carter only having eyes for Jess. 'It's time,' she whispered. 'You're going to regret accepting Carter's invitation to dinner!' Kathy readied herself for bed, an evil smile creeping across her face.

* * *

After breakfast the following morning, Carter went to the cellar while Jess headed to the bar. Seeing her opportunity, Kathy followed Jess, broom in hand. As she swept the floor, she said, 'So Carter's taking you to dinner then.'

'Yes,' Jess replied blandly as she dried the glasses she'd just washed.

'You shouldn't have agreed to go.'

Jess looked up at the girl leaning on the sweeping brush. 'Why not?'

''Cos he ain't for you,' Kathy replied with a glare.

'Well, that remains to be seen.' Jess began to feel a little uncomfortable at the way the conversation was going.

'Tell him you'm not interested.'

'What? Why would I do that?' Now Jess was decidedly uneasy. Kathy's expression was set firm and there was an evil glint in her eye.

'If you don't, you might find the coppers paying a visit to your friend, Jim.'

Jess gasped and her hands began to shake. 'Kathy, why are you saying this?'

'Carter was mine before you came, and I'm gonna make sure

you can't have him!' Kathy snarled. 'Now if you don't want Jim arrested for murder – you know what to do.' Not waiting for an answer, Kathy strode from the room.

Jess stared after her with an open mouth. The cleaner had openly blackmailed her without so much as a by-your-leave.

Placing the glass on the counter, Jess forced her mind back to when she first arrived. Had Kathy and Carter been in a relationship then? She didn't think so and she couldn't remember ever seeing anything to convince her otherwise. Clearly Kathy was in love with Carter but Jess felt certain the girl's feelings were not, nor had ever been, reciprocated.

Jess knew she couldn't risk Kathy carrying out her threat to inform the police about Jim killing Bill, so there was only one option open to her. She had to tell Carter she'd changed her mind, otherwise Jim Butler would end up in jail, or worse.

Hearing whistling coming from the cellar, Jess's eyes welled with tears. Just when she thought there was a chance of happiness for her, it had been snatched away in an instant. She couldn't bear seeing the look of disappointment on Carter's face when she told him she wasn't going out with him. How could she spend every day with him knowing she couldn't be with him? It would be unbearable. There was only one option – she would have to leave the pub.

Where would I go? she wondered. She couldn't go back to the house in Brick Kiln Croft as it was rented, and would most probably have a new family in it now. She could try for a job in another pub somewhere; she could even go back to Wednesbury. The thought didn't thrill her, after all, she'd made a new life for herself here in Birmingham. *Whatever am I to do?* Jess covered her face with her hands before slamming them on the counter. She needed to speak to someone about this – but who?

Suddenly an idea popped into her head. Taking off her

apron, she threw it on the bar and rushed to the kitchen. Seeing Kathy drinking tea, Jess glared her dislike of the woman.

'Have you seen Ellen?' she asked Gail.

'She's in her office,' the cook responded.

Jess smiled at Kathy and was pleased to see a look of uncertainty pass across the girl's face. *She thinks I'm going to tell Ellen about the blackmail. Well, let her worry about it for a while.*

Going to the office, Jess tapped on the door and walked in. 'Ellen, I'm taking a couple of hours off. I have something to do which can't wait.'

'All right, love. Can I help with...?' Ellen began.

'No, but thanks. I'll be back later.' Jess went to her room and grabbed her bag. Unscrewing the brass knob of her bedstead, she felt inside and pulled out some money which she shoved in her bag and ran downstairs.

Outside she hailed a cab and asked to be taken to the railway station. Jess knew exactly who to discuss her problem with.

* * *

Back at The Queen's Head, Kathy was fretting. Jess had gone to Ellen's office and hadn't come out as yet. Was Ellen being informed of the conversation between Jess and herself earlier in the bar?

Kathy began to sweat. Even with the back door propped open, not a breath of air stirred the heat of the kitchen. She was becoming agitated at not knowing what was going on in the office.

Carter came up from the cellar. 'Blimey, it's hot in here!'

'I have to have the range going if you want your lunch,' Gail explained.

Carter dropped onto a kitchen chair and, feeling the teapot, he nodded before he poured himself a cup of tea.

Kathy eyed him across the table, taking in his muscular arms, his dark hair and his brown eyes. This handsome man was destined to become hers.

I'll see you in hell, Jess Lacey, before I'll let you steal him from me! she thought as she sipped her own tea.

21

The train carriage was swelteringly hot and Jess fanned her face with her ticket. Children were whining and crying and people were crushed together on the wooden seating.

'What's up with you now?' a woman asked her snivelling child.

'I'm thirsty,' the boy replied.

'Well, you'll 'ave to wait 'til we get home,' his mother said. 'Now shut yer grizzling before I give you summat to cry about.' The boy sat on the floor with a scowl and crossed his ankles and his arms in disgust. Looking at Jess, the woman said, 'Kids! Never bloody satisfied.'

Jess gave what she thought was a sympathetic smile then looked out of the window.

The train sped past houses, heathland then more buildings, but Jess didn't register them; her mind was occupied elsewhere.

Eventually the train halted and Jess alighted, glad of the breeze blowing along the platform. Out on the street, she hailed a cab. The walk to Brick Kiln Croft would have been nice in the sunshine, but Jess was in a hurry. She needed to speak to her friend about Kathy's threat to report Peg's husband to the police.

Paying the cabbie, Jess walked to the back of number twenty-four and, banging on the door, she let herself in. 'Peg, it's me, Jess,' she called out, closing the door behind her.

'Hello, love, I'm in the living room. What a lovely surprise! What brings you here?'

Jess went through and hugged her friend, who was looking much better after her ordeal. 'How are you?' she asked.

'I'm all right, healing nicely. Cup of tea?'

'I'll do it, you stay there.' Jess went to the kitchen and busied herself.

'There's cake on the cold slab,' Peg called.

Once they were settled with refreshments, Jess began. 'We have a cleaner at the pub called Kathy...' Peg nodded instantly, knowing something was wrong. 'Oh, Peg, she's blackmailing me!' Jess gushed.

'All right, tell me – from the beginning,' Peg said calmly.

Once Jess had got to the end of the sorry tale, Peg blew out her cheeks. 'This Kathy sounds like a nasty piece of work.'

Jess nodded. 'I had no idea until this morning. She's always kept herself to herself. I'm worried for Jim and his pals, I don't want her opening her big mouth.'

'I can see that, but you can't allow her to threaten you either. You have a chance to be happy at last, Jess, and you cannot let this woman get in the way of that!'

'I don't know what else to do though, Peg!'

'First thing, go outside and find a runner.'

Jess frowned but did as she was bid. Out on the street, she glanced around.

'Need help, Mrs Lacey?'

Jess saw the old man with his walking stick hobbling down his path opposite her.

'I'm looking for a runner, Mr Appleby,' she said.

Putting two fingers in his mouth, the old fellow whistled loudly.

'Thank you,' she said.

'I was the one who fetched Jim from work the day your husband battered Mrs Butler,' he informed her.

'That was very kind of you,' Jess said as a dirty boy ran towards them, his bare feet slapping the road as he came.

'You after me, missus?' the boy asked.

'Yes, come with me. Thanks, Mr Appleby.' Jess led the boy indoors.

'Right, lad. Do you know where they'm building the new houses up past St Peter's Church?' Peg asked. At the boy's nod, she went on. 'I need you to sprint over there and tell Jim Butler his wife needs him.'

'Okay,' the boy said, eyeing the cake.

Peg found a halfpenny in her apron pocket. She passed over the coin then cut a generous slice of cake and handed it to the runner.

'Ta, missus.' With that, the lad shot out of the house.

'The runners are a handy messenger service,' Peg said with a smile.

'Won't Jim get into trouble for leaving work early?'

'Nah, his boss thinks the world of him, and after what happened to me...'

'Peg, I'm so sorry.'

'Jess, you've no need to apologise, it wasn't you who did it and besides, the bugger's gone now.'

While they waited, Jess regaled her friend with the tale of Bella knocking Flint out cold.

They were still laughing when Jim rushed in. 'What's happened?' he asked breathlessly.

'We have a problem, sweetheart. I think you'd better sit down.'

Jess explained again about Kathy's threat and when she'd finished, Jim said, 'I suppose it was too much to ask for everyone to keep their mouths shut.'

'I'll have to do as she asks, otherwise you could end up in prison!'

'Now don't be hasty, there's a solution to every problem – we just have to find it.'

'But Jim...!' Jess began.

'Hush now and let me think.' Jim rubbed his chin and pondered. After a while he asked, 'Can you postpone your outing with Carter for – say a week?'

'Yes, I suppose so, but why?'

'We need the time to come up with some ideas.'

'I could say I don't feel well.'

'Excellent! The rest you can leave to me.'

'What do you have in mind?' Jess asked.

'I can't say just now but be assured I'll sort it out.'

'Thanks, Jim, I'm sorry to have brought this to your door but I thought you should know.'

'Don't you worry about a thing. All you have to do for now is be poorly on Wednesday.'

22

In compliance with Jim's instructions, Jess feigned illness on Wednesday morning. She began to cough at breakfast and, with her elbow on the table, she rested her head in her hand.

'Are you all right, Jess?' Carter asked.

'In truth, I'm feeling unwell. Would you mind if we cancelled this evening?'

'Of course not. Maybe you should go back to bed.'

'Yes, I think I will.' Jess got to her feet and glanced at Kathy who, with a smirk on her face, nodded.

Jess went to her room, wondering how long she would have to keep up the charade. Going to the window, she looked out onto the street at the folks ambling past. It was early but already hot so she pushed up the sash window and leaned out. Houses and front-room shops lined the street on both sides and Jess eyed the comings and goings of women as they sauntered along, looking at the wares on offer. Men strode out, their hobnailed boots tapping a rhythm on the cobblestones, their flat caps shielding their heads from the sun and shirtsleeves rolled up above the elbows.

The dray cart arrived and she watched the beer barrels being unloaded and rolled down the ramp into the cellar. Carter pushed out the empty ones which were stacked on the cart. She heard him whistling before he closed the doors set into the street.

She thought about Jim and what his plan was but she had no idea, leaving her thoroughly frustrated. Kathy clearly thought she had the better of Jess, which of course at the moment she did. How would she feel in the end when Jim bested her?

Although not really poorly, Jess was tired. She hadn't slept well since speaking with Peg and Jim, and not knowing the plan left her feeling useless and blaming herself for everything that had happened.

A knock on her door made her jump and, going to open it, she saw Ellen with a tray. 'I thought you might like a cuppa,' Ellen said as she walked in and laid the tray on the dressing table.

'Thanks, Ellen,' Jess said, sitting on her bed.

'Do you want to tell me what's going on?' Ellen asked.

'Pardon?'

'Jess, I know you're not ill so why did you cancel your evening out with Carter?'

'Ellen, it's complicated.'

'Have you changed your mind about him?'

'No!' Jess answered. 'No, it's just – I don't know how to explain it.'

'All right, I won't push you, but I'll be in the office if you need me.' Ellen left the room, closing the door with a quiet click.

Jess dragged her hands over her face then went to pour the tea.

* * *

Down in the kitchen, Carter asked, 'How is Jess feeling now?'

'I don't think she's ill at all,' Ellen answered.

'What do you mean?' Gail posed the question.

'There's nothing wrong with her physically. Something has happened in the last couple of days which has that girl scared out of her wits.'

'What?' Gail asked.

'I don't know,' Ellen said.

No, but I do! Kathy touched the coin in her skirt pocket yet again, a satisfied smile on her lips. *So, Lacey, you didn't tell Ellen after all.*

Ellen retired to her office while the others got to work.

In the cellar, Carter pondered Ellen's words as he dragged the newly delivered barrels into place. What could have occurred to have Jess so frightened? With no answer forthcoming, he swept the floor, trying not to worry. Not fretting was an impossible task, he decided after only a moment, so, putting the broom away, he returned to the kitchen.

'Gail, have you any idea what's wrong with Jess?' he asked.

'No, but I think it's very strange.'

Kathy sipped her tea and listened.

'I do as well,' Carter admitted.

'Maybe her husband's murder is playing on her mind and she feels guilty,' Kathy said quietly.

'Why would she? She didn't do it!' Carter responded sharply.

'No, but she was the cause of it all.' Kathy's words made Carter and Gail exchange a look which acknowledged that the cleaner might be right.

'Why would she cancel our evening out though?' Carter was perturbed at not having the answers, and at Gail's shake of her head, he ran a hand through his hair and sighed with frustration.

'If you still want to go, I'll come with you,' Kathy said.

Carter looked at her, saying, 'No, it's all right, I'm sure once all this is sorted out Jess and I can rearrange.'

Kathy was cut to the quick at his remark and scowled fiercely.

Carter didn't notice – but Gail did, and after Kathy left the kitchen she pointed it out. 'You've upset Kathy now, and you know what else? I think she loves you and is jealous of you and Jess.'

'Surely not?' he asked. 'We hardly talk to each other.'

Gail said, 'You should be careful around that one – in fact we all should.'

'Why do you say that?'

'Because,' Gail answered, 'our secret may not be quite as secure as we thought.'

Carter glanced at the doorway through which Kathy had disappeared then back to the cook. Her slow nod affirmed his sudden concern. 'Bloody hell!'

'I couldn't agree more, Mr Adams. The question now is – what do we do about it?'

Carter slumped, having no idea how to answer.

23

Over in Wednesbury, dressed in her best clothes, Peg left the house. As she walked down the street, she thought about the town she lived in. In the heart of the Black Country in middle England, Wednesbury was known for its nail making and tube making. There were wheelwrights, coopers and blacksmiths dotted all over, and at night the forges opened their doors, casting red light from the fires which could be seen for miles. Streets and houses were lit by gas which the council were hoping to convert to electricity before too long.

Steam tram cars passed through the marketplace, ferrying passengers to their destinations. The new railway station, built in 1862, now had a branch to the nearby town of Darlaston. Birmingham Canal was cut to link Wednesbury and Birmingham industries, and steam trams were now opened to Dudley and Tipton. Two years previously, in 1887, Brunswick Park had opened to celebrate Queen Victoria's golden jubilee.

Peg strode on, glancing at the grimy buildings where coal dust from the pits clung to the brickwork. For all the modern trappings the town could boast, there was still a great deal of poverty. Jobs were hard to come by and men stood on street corners in what was known as the *bread line*. Here they waited, day in, day out, hoping to be given work by employers looking for workers. Once chosen, these men would earn a copper or two which would then put bread on the table for their families, hence its sobriquet.

Women visited the market late at night as the stall holders were packing up. That was the best time to find a bargain on meat and vegetables. Vendors would sell off their products very cheaply so they didn't have to carry them home.

Children scavenged, praying they would find a dropped coin or be given some bread or fruit.

Coming to the market, Peg began at one end, weaving her way between the stalls. The place was packed with people looking for a bargain and Peg kept her bag tucked safely under her arm rather than give a pick-pocket an easy target.

Stopping at each stall, Peg asked around if anyone knew of any jobs going begging. No one did, and she moved on. She passed flower vendors, a woman's barrow with second-hand children's clothes, a bread and cake cart, and a man selling crockery who piled cups into tall towers, making everyone gasp.

'How do, Peg?' a woman called.

'Hello, Flo,' she replied.

''Ere, you got out of the hospital at the right time, d'aint yer?'

Everyone had heard about Peg's injuries and they all sympathised. Bill Lacey hadn't been well liked and they all knew what a brute he was.

'Why's that then, Flo?'

''Cos they'm up to their eyeballs with diphtheria cases.'

'Blimey, there's always summat. Do you know of anywhere looking for workers?'

'No, bab, sorry.'

Peg gave her thanks and walked on, thinking, *Jim was right, this isn't going to be easy.*

All day she searched, trying shops and factories, but to no avail. No one was hiring. Disconsolately she shuffled her way home, feeling exhausted and demoralised.

That evening, Jim didn't say *I told you so.* Instead he suggested she try the big houses, maybe a housekeeper position might be available. Reading his newspaper later, he didn't hold out much hope for his wife, who had no training of any sort. All he could do was let her come to the realisation on her own – Peg Butler was unlikely to be a working woman any time soon.

'The fellas are coming round later,' Jim called out, 'we need a plan pulling together.'

From the kitchen, Peg replied, 'Tea's up.'

Jim joined her and they sat to their meal of pork chops, potatoes and vegetables covered in thick gravy. 'What are you gonna do?' she asked.

'I dunno but we need to decide – and quick. None of us are safe until we sort out that cleaner at the pub. One word from her and we could all end up in jail.'

'You ain't gonna kill 'er, are you?' Peg asked nervously.

'No, it shouldn't come that. Hopefully we can frighten her off.'

Swallowing her food, Peg said, 'She knows what you did to Bill and she's still blackmailing Jess! I don't think she'll scare that easy.'

'Hmm,' was all Jim managed whilst chewing.

A little later, George, Harry and Bert arrived. Peg provided refreshments and the discussion began. Jim related what Peg had said earlier about the cleaner not being frightened off and the men nodded their agreement.

'So how are we to resolve this?' George asked.

'I'm buggered if I know,' Bert put in.

'Clearly she ain't worried about us coming after her or else she wouldn't be threatening Jess,' Harry supplied.

'We can't do her in – she's a woman!' Bert said.

The little coterie looked at each other, all at a loss as to how to solve the problem.

'You can't frighten her off, Jim, 'cos if you threaten her she'll go straight round the cop shop and flap her lips,' Peg said.

'I told Jess to leave it to us,' Jim said, 'so we have to do something.'

George scratched his head, Bert rubbed his chin and Harry stared at his shoes. With a sigh, Peg got up to put the kettle to boil once more. This was going to take quite a time to work out and a lot of tea would be needed.

* * *

Over at The Queen's Head, Jess had fretted the day away up in her room. As time passed, she became more and more agitated. She couldn't see a way out of the situation she found herself in, and she knew Carter and the others were worried. She couldn't pretend to be ill forever. Even after she recovered from her pretend illness, she would still have to face them all. Carter would expect her to dine out with him at some point and if she kept refusing he would think she had lost interest in him. This would cause tension in the bar and it could lead to her having to leave after all.

It was no use, she couldn't hide up here forever, so, taking a deep breath, she went downstairs.

'There you are, how are you feeling?' Gail asked as Jess entered the kitchen.

'I'm all right, thank you.'

'You ain't, though, are you?' Gail pushed. 'Look, Jess, I think I know what's going on.' Jess looked up with frightened eyes. 'It has to do with Carter and Kathy, am I right?' Jess's eyes flicked to the doorway to the bar where Carter was working and Kathy was sitting drinking gin. 'That look says it all,' Gail went on. 'Is Kathy threatening you with the coppers regarding Bill's death?' Jess nodded, her eyes swimming with tears. 'I guessed as much. That girl's trouble. In fact, I mentioned it to Carter and told him to watch his back.'

'I don't know what to do. Jim knows and he said to leave it with him, but...'

'She won't end up like your husband, Jess, I'm certain.'

Jess, however, was not so sure.

24

After lock-up, Carter and Kathy were both surprised to see Jess sitting in the kitchen. Dropping a hand on her shoulder, Carter asked how she was. Kathy curled her lip like a dog protecting a bone at the overt display of affection.

Ellen joined them and Gail served tea and cake. Assuring everyone she would be fit to work tomorrow, Jess stayed to chat with Gail as Carter and Ellen went to their beds. Kathy soon pretended to follow but really she lay in wait for Jess at the top of the dark stairs.

A little while later, Jess plodded up the staircase and was about to enter her room when a voice made her jump almost out of her skin.

'You'm doing well.'

'What are you after now, Kathy? I did what you asked.' Jess sighed.

'I need some money,' Kathy replied.

'You have your wages, as do all of us.'

'Ar, but I want more. I want yours.'

'No! I draw the line at giving you my hard-earned cash,' Jess said forcefully.

'Fine. Tell Ellen I'll be at the police station in the morning so I won't be able to clean the bar.' Kathy made to walk away.

'Wait!' Jess's harsh whisper cut through the shadows. 'How much do you want?'

'All of it. Every penny, every week.'

'I'll be working for nothing!' Jess was horrified at the thought.

'It's your choice – give up the money or your friend's husband will go to prison. Goodnight.' Kathy walked silently along the corridor, disappearing into the darkness like an apparition.

Jess trudged into her room, tears rolling down her face.

Neither woman had seen or heard Gail approach and wait quietly on the small landing where the stairs turned back on themselves. Nodding to herself, Gail had listened and heard every word.

Very early the following morning, Gail asked to see Ellen, in private. Ensconced in the office, Gail said, 'I know why Jess has been poorly!'

'Tell me,' Ellen urged.

Gail, in quiet whispers, related the conversation she'd overheard on the stairs the previous night.

Ellen's mouth opened wide with the telling before she said, 'I'm aghast that Kathy would do such a thing. I know she can be miserable and sarcastic, but this...!'

'I'm pretty sure this all started over Carter,' Gail informed her employer and friend.

'What does he have to do with it?'

'Blimey, Ellen, you're slow this morning! Kathy is in love with him.'

'Ah, and now she's blaming Jess for getting in the way...'

'Yes!'

'Let me be clear – Kathy and Carter weren't in a relationship before though.'

'No, but I think Kathy wishes they were.'

Ellen sat back in her chair and sighed loudly. 'What are we going to do with this knowledge?'

Gail shook her head. 'Another question is – do we tell Carter? And...'

'And what?'

'Do we tell Jess we know?'

Ellen pondered a moment then posed yet another question. 'Does Jim know?'

'I believe so, I think that's where Jess went the other day, to tell him. I think a meeting with Jess might be a good idea so we can thrash this out once and for all.'

'I agree, but we need to be careful. I'll tell you what, if you bring me a cup of tea please you can ask Jess – quietly – to join us.'

'Good idea.' Gail got to her feet and left the office.

In the kitchen, Jess had just made a fresh pot of tea and was pouring as Gail walked in.

'I'll take Ellen a cup,' Gail said.

'I can do it, I don't mind,' Jess replied, preparing a tray.

Gail watched her go then said, 'I need the privy.'

Unsuspectingly, Kathy sipped her drink, ignoring the cook, she had eyes only for Carter.

Gail hurried to the office and closed the door behind her. Then an in-depth discussion began, which brought everyone up to date with the goings-on.

Jess sighed with relief that she didn't have to carry her burden alone any more and all knew of her plight. 'Jim and

Peg are aware, and Jim said to leave it to him to find a solution.'

'He's in enough trouble, Jess, especially if ever it should get out about the truth of your husband's demise,' Ellen said.

'The only option left open to me then is to pay Kathy and hope she keeps her mouth shut,' Jess responded glumly.

'No, there has to be a way out of this where you don't give in to her blackmail!' Gail said in a forceful whisper.

'Well, I'm all out of ideas,' Ellen said. 'For the present go back to work and keep an eye on Kathy.' Then, in a moment of inspiration, she added, 'I'm going to call you in one by one because I'm about to give you each a rise in wages. That way I can inform Carter without making Kathy suspicious.'

'Clever. I'd best go, I'm supposed to be in the privy,' Gail said before rushing back to the kitchen.

'You've been a long time,' Kathy said when Gail returned.

'Yes, I know. I think I need some prunes.'

'Ar, that'll do the trick,' Kathy concurred, wrinkling her brow in disgust.

'Ladies, do you mind? I'm trying to enjoy my brew,' Carter said.

Jess appeared at the kitchen door. 'Carter, Ellen would like to see you.'

'Right,' he said and off he went.

'What's going on?' Kathy asked.

'I've no idea,' Jess lied.

Ten minutes passed before Carter came back, saying, 'Kathy, Ellen wants you.'

With a frown, the cleaner got to her feet and shuffled out.

As soon as she'd gone, Carter whispered, 'Jess, why didn't you tell me?'

'I didn't know how.'

'Well, this evening you and I are going to Wednesbury. It's time to have a meeting with your friend, Peg, and her husband. Ellen will stand the bar with Gail's help. It's all agreed.'

'That's fine by me,' Gail said as she slapped bacon rashers into a large frying pan.

'Gail, Ellen's asking for you,' Kathy said, coming into the room. 'It seems we'm all having a wage increase,' she added after Gail had gone.

Jess took over the cooking as Carter asked, 'Kathy, I wonder if you could do me a favour.'

'O'course,' the cleaner replied, with a smirk in Jess's direction.

'Could you cook this evening? Gail and Ellen are tending the bar.'

'What about her?' she asked, pointing to Jess.

'Jess and I have to go out. We have an errand to run for Ellen.'

'What errand?'

'It's not up to me to say. If Ellen wants you to know, she'll tell you herself.'

'Fine!' Kathy yelled and stamped from the room, grabbing her broom as she went. Sweeping the bar, she muttered under her breath. 'There's summat going on here and I aim to find out what it is. Treat me like dirt they do, giving me the shit jobs to do, treating me like a skivvy. I don't 'ave to put up with it, you know, I can leave whenever I want...'

The more she mumbled, the louder she got until she was shouting.

Gail and Ellen rushed to see what all the noise was and were shocked at the cleaner smacking the furniture with her sweeping brush.

'This is all down to you, Jess Lacey!' Kathy yelled as the

brush head hit a tabletop. 'You steal my man and this is what you'll get!' Again and again the brush hit the table until with a final blow the broom shattered. 'Oops,' Kathy said with a little giggle.

Exchanging glances, everyone was of the same opinion. Kathy Frith had gone quite mad.

25

Peg Butler set out yet again looking for work. She was determined and had no intention of giving up until she was in employment. Walking along Lower High Street, she stopped to look into a dress shop window before going inside.

'Good morning, I'll be with you in a moment,' a saleswoman called out to her.

Peg nodded and watched as a woman was sashaying about in a voluminous gown. Pink tulle over a half-hoop petticoat, the waist was supposed to be nipped in but didn't quite fit the form it adorned. The neckline was a little too low, showing more flesh than was proper, and Peg ground her teeth together rather than speak out of turn.

'It's perfect for you,' the modiste gushed.

'I'm not sure...' the customer began.

'It's in your price range.'

Peg stood and without realising she started to shake her head. The customer caught the movement as she looked into the long mirror. Turning, she asked Peg, 'What do you think?'

'It's not for me to say.'

'Please give me your opinion,' the woman insisted.

'Well, I would suggest something a little younger for you.'

'Really?' The woman glanced again in the looking glass. 'Yes, I think you're right, but what?'

Peg looked around and spotted a white dress with a ruffle hem. 'That, maybe?'

'I'm afraid that's a lot more expensive,' the saleswoman said.

'No matter, I'll try it.'

Moments later, the customer emerged from the changing room, a vision in white, and rushed to the mirror. 'Oh, yes! This is much better!' Turning to Peg once more, she held out her arms.

'Most definitely,' Peg said, 'it brings out the English rose in you.'

'Thank you!' To the modiste, the woman said, 'I'll take it.' With that she went to the dressing room to change.

Having paid her money, the happy customer left the shop clutching her box under her arm.

'Thank you for your input,' the modiste said, 'that was a good sale. Now what can I do for you?'

'I came to ask for a job,' Peg replied bluntly.

'My name is Amelia Prescott. Come with me.'

'Peg Butler, pleased to meet you.'

Amelia took Peg to the office and asked her to sit. 'Now, Peg, tell me about yourself.'

'I'm married to Jim; we have no children but not through choice. My closest friend recently moved away and I'm lonely so I thought I would try for work. Jim provides well for us so it's not that I need the money, it's more the company I'm seeking.'

'Well, you certainly seem to know how to sell and you clearly have an eye for fashion. Look, I tell you what, I'll give you a trial today and see how you get on. If I'm happy by the end of the day then you can have a job, because I could do with the help, I have to admit. How does that sound?'

'That sounds marvellous.' Peg beamed.

'All the stock is marked up with a price ticket so there's no dispute with customers. Can you use a till?'

'I'll only need showing once,' Peg said with a grin.

'You can leave your bag in the drawer in the desk. Through that door is the kitchen and the privy is in the yard. Any questions?' Peg shook her head. 'You haven't asked about wages.'

'Like I said, it's the company I want but a wage would be a bonus.'

The little bell over the shop door interrupted their conversation. 'Right, Peg, your first customer awaits,' Amelia said with a smile as she ushered Peg into the shop area.

'Good morning, madam, miss.' Peg addressed the mother and daughter. 'How can Amelia's be of service to you today?'

'We're looking for a coming-out dress for Francine,' the woman pointed to her daughter, 'she's being presented next weekend.'

It was the custom for wealthy families to present their daughters into society at a ball or party once reaching a certain age, usually seventeen or eighteen.

'How exciting!' Peg said enthusiastically. 'May I ask if you have anything particular in mind?'

'Not too revealing but otherwise...' Mother replied.

Peg looked at Amelia for guidance. 'You might want to show our customers this range,' Amelia said, leading the women to a long line of dresses on a rail against the back wall. Then she stood back and watched.

'Ooh, Mummy, I like this one!' the girl whose name was Francine said breathlessly as she touched a pale blue chiffon gown.

Seeing the mother frown, Peg stepped in. 'Maybe something in white for your presentation,' she said, pulling out a tulle dress. 'It's a momentous occasion and must be celebrated with the finest of attire.'

Francine's mother smiled and so did Amelia.

'Hmm. I wanted something a little more...' Francine began.

'Grown up?' Peg asked. Seeing the nod, Peg replaced the gown and pulled out another. 'Now this is most definitely you, if I may say so.'

Amelia held her breath for a moment; the dress was one of the most expensive in the shop.

Holding the garment in front of the girl by the mirror, Peg said, 'With your lovely dark hair up in curls and a delicate necklace I think you will certainly turn heads. Would you care to try it?'

'Yes, please,' came the excited reply.

In the fitting room, Peg helped the girl into the dress and finding a few clips she gathered up her dark hair and pinned it in place. 'Let's see what your mother thinks,' Peg suggested, leading Francine out to where her mother was waiting.

'Oh, my goodness! Francine, you look beautiful, and it fits so well!'

'It does, doesn't it, Mummy.' Going to the mirror, she turned this way and that so the full chiffon skirt swished around her legs. Above the nipped-in waist sat a bodice with capped sleeves. Although the neckline was low, it was still modest. 'I love it! Please say I can have it, Mummy – please!'

'Are you sure that's the one you want?'

'Yes, Mummy!'

'Jolly good, we'll take it.'

As Peg and Francine returned to the dressing room, Amelia smiled broadly.

Moments later, Peg led her customer back to her parent and then went to box the gown. Removing the price tag, she showed the mother, whose eyebrows shot up in surprise but with a resigned nod she gave Peg leave to continue. Handing over the money, mother and daughter left with effusive thanks.

Amelia showed Peg how to work the till and in went the money. 'Well done, Peg!' Amelia said. 'I can't believe it; I've been trying to shift that dress for ages!'

'Glad to be of help. Now, should I make us both a cuppa?'

Amelia laughed. 'That settles it – you have the job! Welcome to Amelia's, Peg.'

'Thank you.' Hardly able to contain her excitement, Peg went to familiarise herself with the kitchen.

Enjoying their hot beverage, Amelia said, 'Regarding wages, how does ten shillings a week sound?'

Peg gaped at the amount. 'Bloody marvellous!'

The two were still laughing when the shop bell tinkled again.

26

Whilst Peg was being inducted into the world of fashion, over in Birmingham the staff at The Queen's Head were gaping at Kathy and her broken brush.

Ellen ventured carefully into the bar, saying, 'Kathy love, I think it's time for a new broom.'

'Ar, because this one is bosted.' Kathy picked up the broken bits of wood and walked past Ellen like nothing had happened. Depositing the pieces in the scullery, she called out, 'I'll go down the market and fetch another.'

Everyone in the kitchen watched Kathy leave the pub by the back door then sat with pure relief to discuss the cleaner's outburst. Gail removed the pan from the hotplate and set it aside; breakfast could wait a while.

'I've never seen anything like it!' Ellen said.

'Kathy has it in for you, Jess, that's for sure,' Gail added.

'I don't understand. I've given her no encouragement,' Carter said.

'Well, she seems to be convinced you belong to her,' Jess replied.

'It's like she's two different people in the same body,' Gail put in. 'She changed just like that!' She clicked her fingers.

'What do we do now?' Ellen asked. 'Because in my opinion Kathy is unstable.'

'Which makes her unreliable. She could be spilling all our secrets as we speak!' Jess said, becoming agitated.

'You two get over to Peg's right now, we can't wait until this evening,' Ellen suggested as she nodded at Carter and Jess.

'Jim will be at work,' Jess reminded the others.

'Then go and see him there!' Ellen blasted.

The couple got to their feet and rushed from the room to change out of their work clothes. Then they set off, leaving Ellen and Gail to deal with Kathy on her return from the market.

Carter whistled for a cab and, once inside, Jess said, 'I'm so sorry.'

'What for?'

'Bringing all this trouble to your door,' she replied.

'It's not your fault, Jess. It seems Kathy thinks she and I should be an item. She's clearly very jealous of you.'

'She is, isn't she? I don't know where this has all come from. I'm not sure why we're going to see Jim though. I don't see how he can help.'

'You never know, he could have some ideas as to how we can sort this mess out. Besides, it will alert him to be ready to flee should the need arise.'

'Oh, Carter, do you think it might come to that...?'

'No, but it has to be considered.'

Reaching the railway station, Carter paid the cabbie then purchased the train tickets. They walked onto the platform and waited impatiently.

After their rail journey and another cab ride, Jess and Carter finally arrived at Peg's house. Knocking on the back door, Jess tried the handle but she was surprised to find that it was locked. 'That's strange, Peg is usually at home.'

'Maybe she's shopping,' Carter said.

'Let's go and ask Mr Appleby.'

'Who?'

'A neighbour.'

Walking around to the front of the house, Jess saw the old man hobbling down his path. 'She ain't in, Mrs Lacey.'

'So I see, do you know where she's gone?'

'No, but she was dressed up to the nines when she left this morning.'

'Thanks, Mr Appleby.' Turning to Carter, she asked, 'Now what?'

'We go and see Jim.'

'He's working on them new houses by St Peter's Church,' Appleby said helpfully.

With more thanks and a wave, the couple strode away. Crossing the Holyhead Road, they walked along Queen Street, and on past the church and football ground in Lloyd Street which was lined with houses on one side.

Seeing the building site and hearing sawing and banging, Jess said, 'There it is.' As they walked, the sun was hidden by clouds and Jess glanced up. 'Oh, Lord, it's going to rain,' she muttered.

As they arrived at the site, a man said to them, 'Sorry, folks, but you can't be on here, it's dangerous.'

'I'm looking for Jim Butler,' Jess informed him.

The man glanced around then pointed. 'He's up on the roof. Wait there and I'll fetch him.'

Moments later, Jim stood before them and Jess quietly explained what had occurred at the pub. 'We went to the house but Peg wasn't there,' Jess said.

'She'll be out looking for a job,' Jim replied.

'Ah, that would make sense. Apparently she was looking very smart when she left. Mr Appleby told us where you worked.'

'God love the old man, he's our regular neighbourhood watch,' Jim said with a warm smile. Then his expression turned serious once more. 'The lads came round and we thrashed it out, but to no avail. Short of sending that cleaner after Bill, we had no ideas.'

'Jim, no!' Jess gasped.

'I know, I know,' he replied, 'it's the last thing I want to do, but what else can we do?'

'Well, not that, Jim. There's been enough blood shed already. I'm left with no alternative, I'll have to pay her to keep her mouth shut,' Jess said sadly.

'You will not!' Carter's stern words made Jess look up at him. 'Sorry, sweetheart, I didn't mean to be so sharp, but Kathy will never let up – even if you pay her. First she warned you off me, now she wants your money – what next?'

'I don't know.' Jess's eyes filled with tears as she spoke.

'Right, Jim, as of now your involvement in all this must cease. You have to stay well clear of Kathy and remain safe. Somehow we have to deal with this at our end.'

'Okay, Carter, I understand. Good luck and I hope you can find a solution so that all of us can rest a bit easier in our beds.' Jim nodded before he returned to his work with mixed feelings. On the one hand, he wanted to help Jess be free of the worry of paying all of her money over to a blackmailer, but on the other hand he had no idea how to go about it. He watched Jess and Carter walk away, none the wiser for their trip.

* * *

Whilst the pair were making their way home, Kathy had arrived back at the pub with a new broom.

Ellen and Gail watched quietly as Kathy completed her cleaning without so much as a word about what had gone on before. She had not enquired as to the whereabouts of Jess or Carter, seemingly not even noticing they were not there. Then she left the bar and sat, as usual, in the kitchen with a cup of tea. Gail had cooked breakfast for them just after Jess and Carter had left, and she was now busy preparing lunch. Ellen sat at the table also sipping her drink but keeping an eye on Kathy, all the time afraid the girl would blow up again.

It was mid-afternoon by the time the team were back together again, and Jess gave a barely perceptible shake of her head when her eyes met Ellen's. Ellen screwed up her mouth in disappointment; evidently no resolution had been reached.

In order to abide by the drinking laws, The Queen's Head closed its doors between three and five so Jess took the time to restock the bar. Carter retired to the cellar and the others remained in the kitchen.

Kathy stared off into space, seemingly quite normal again after her earlier episode, and no one dared make reference to it. However, they were all sure that the cleaner was a danger to herself and to them and the atmosphere was strained as they all returned to their duties. Kathy appeared oblivious to the anxious mood. When the pub opened its doors to the public once more, Kathy was in her usual seat in the bar, sipping gin and glaring at Jess.

Jess, for her part, tried her best to ignore the eyes boring into her but the uncomfortable feeling hung over her like a shroud. She was very glad when Carter joined her behind the counter.

That night after lock-up and Kathy and Carter had gone to bed, Ellen went to the kitchen and handed Jess some money.

'What's this?' Jess asked.

'To pay Kathy while we try to find a solution.'

'No, Ellen, I can't take it.'

'Jess, I can afford it. This way you won't be working for nothing.'

Gail watched the exchange before saying, 'Take it, Jess, it will give us more time to sort out this sorry situation.'

'I'll borrow it then, thank you, Ellen. With luck we might be able to get it back somehow.'

Ellen nodded her agreement but not at all confident that Jess was right.

The three women went to their beds, feeling wretched that they had a blackmailer in their midst; seemingly something they could do nothing about.

27

As the summer hurried on, Jess received a letter from Peg which she tore open excitedly.

'My friend Peg has found a job! She's working at Amelia's in Lower High Street in Wednesbury.'

'What's Amelia's?' Kathy asked.

'A very nice dress shop,' Ellen put in. 'Expensive but beautiful gowns.'

'I might try it,' Kathy said as she looked at Jess pointedly.

'A dress from there would take all of your wages and more,' Ellen advised.

'I've got savings!' Kathy snapped.

Ellen didn't reply, not wanting to set the cleaner off into another rage.

'Ain't your friend married to Jim?' Kathy asked.

'Yes,' Jess said with sudden trepidation. Why had Kathy asked the question? She knew full well Peg and Jim were husband and wife.

Jess glanced at Ellen, knowing they were both thinking the

same thing. Was Kathy about to take her blackmail a step further – to Peg?

Seeing the worried look on Jess's face, Kathy knew her words had struck a chord. 'Right, I'll start upstairs,' the cleaner said, getting to her feet.

When she'd gone, Gail whispered, 'Jess, you really should be more careful what you say in front of Kathy.'

'I know but I was just so pleased for Peg,' she replied.

'Looking at your faces, I reckon we have all come to the same conclusion,' Carter put in. 'Peg could become Kathy's second victim.'

'Oh, Lord!' Jess exclaimed.

'Write to Peg and warn her,' Ellen said.

'I will.'

'Do it now before Kathy makes any plans,' Ellen insisted. Jess nodded and stood to leave the kitchen. 'Jess, write your letter in the office so Kathy won't see you and want to know what you're doing.'

'Good idea, thanks, Ellen.' Jess raced off to complete her task.

'This is getting out of hand,' Carter said quietly.

Gail and Ellen nodded. 'She'll try it on with us next,' Gail said as a throwaway remark.

'Good grief!' Carter gasped. 'Ellen, if we're not careful she could try to steal every penny you have! And if you become a pauper what will happen to you and all the unfortunate women you help?'

'I'm sure it won't come to that, Carter. But as much as I hate to say it, something has to be done about Kathy – and soon,' Ellen replied.

Upstairs, Kathy was supposed to be cleaning Jess's room but in actual fact she was searching it. Jess kept her money somewhere and Kathy wanted to find it. If she could steal Jess's savings it would leave the girl unable to pay her blackmail money. If that was the case, Jess would have to borrow from someone else and Kathy had decided she would then double what she'd asked for. Then a quick trip to Wednesbury to have a word with Peg could see her even more well off. Kathy had no qualms about blackmailing Peg as well. It was her husband who had committed murder, after all, and Peg would want to keep him safe so she was sure to pay up.

Lifting the mattress, Kathy looked beneath it but found nothing. She searched the wardrobe and drawers too. Where on earth was Jess hiding her money? Leaving the room, Kathy was frustrated at being thwarted, but she determined she would find the money sooner or later.

Later that night, Jess wearily climbed the stairs to bed. Reaching the landing, a voice stopped her in her tracks. 'Time to pay up.'

Jess swung around to face Kathy. 'If I give you all of my money...'

'I don't want a sob story, I just want your wages, so come on, hand 'em over.'

Jess reached into her apron pocket and pulled out the money Ellen had given her.

Kathy snatched it, saying, 'Same time next week.' Then she made for her room, laughing as she went.

A moment later, Gail appeared.

'I paid her,' Jess whispered.

'I heard. We have to sort this out soon or we could all be giving her our cash.'

'That's what I'm afraid of. Oh, Gail, I don't know what to do!'

'Let's go into your room in case we're overheard,' Gail suggested.

Once in the bedroom with the door firmly closed, the two women spoke in hushed tones. 'I'm scared, Gail. Kathy could blackmail Peg, you, Ellen...'

'That's my fear as well. Oh, and another thought – hide your money well because I think our cleaner has been snooping through my things.'

'How do you know?' Jess asked, horrified at the idea.

'Little things like my underwear was not how I left it in the drawer, and my shoes were in the wrong place in the wardrobe.'

'She's not even being careful about it then,' Jess said. 'Does Ellen know?'

'Yes. I had a quick word when I took her tea to the office. I've taken to carrying my money with me because I can't find a safe enough place to stash it.'

'I keep mine here,' Jess said, unscrewing the knob on her bedframe and pulling out what remained of her savings.

'That's a good idea, I think I'll do the same,' Gail said. 'Right, bed for me. Try to get some sleep. We'll sort this, one way or the other.'

After Gail left, Jess went to the window and stared out into the dark night.

Everything had been so good when she had first arrived and now it was all going wrong. Jess knew she wouldn't have been in this position had Bill not assaulted Peg. His actions had not only led to his death, but also to Kathy's blackmail.

Even from the grave, Bill was still taunting her; determined to ruin her happiness.

28

Peg settled into her new job happily and quickly became familiar with the materials, designs and prices of all the garments on sale. Amelia Prescott was delighted with her new assistant who was pleasant, polite and a big hit with the customers. Dresses were flying out of the shop, as were skirts and blouses, and Amelia ordered more stock including more hats. Despite it still being summer, the new range would be for autumn. For now, however, cotton and silk garments were selling well.

'Peg, how would you like to change the window display?' Amelia asked.

'I'd love to. Did you have anything in mind?'

'No, I'll leave it up to you. Enjoy yourself!'

Peg scrambled into the window space, suddenly feeling on show to the public. Stripping the window completely, she then went to the racks. Pulling out a white cotton dress, she slipped it onto the mannequin. Adding little lacy gloves and a boater, she set it to the left of the space. An open parasol was placed over the dummy and tied to one hand with fine thread, the other end of the thread was secured to the window frame with drawing pins holding it in place. Another mannequin was dressed in pale pink chiffon with a teardrop hat and matching gloves. A closed parasol was hooked over the dummy's arm so that the two looked as though they were out for a stroll. On the other side of the space, Peg set up some boxes at different heights and draped them with a length of lemon silk. Here she positioned hats, gloves and parasols.

Smiling and waving to passers-by, Peg worked tirelessly, arranging everything in just the right places. People stopped to watch her and every now and then someone would enter the shop to make a purchase.

Finally, hot and tired, Peg climbed out of the window and went outside to view her handiwork.

'Very nice,' a woman said as she walked past.

Peg gave her thanks but felt something was still missing. Going back indoors, she rifled through the bolts of cloth. Finding what she was searching for, she carried two pieces of brown silk back into the display space. Pinning one each side behind the mannequins and boxes at the top of the frame, she let them fall to the floor.

Going outside again, she smiled; the brown material resembled open doors through which the dummies had just walked.

Amelia joined her and laughed. 'That's very clever, Peg, a shop within a shop!'

They went back indoors, Peg beaming at the compliment.

All afternoon, women stopped to gaze at the new display and business was brisk. By closing time, Peg was exhausted. She wandered home in the sunshine, happy at having done a good job and also pleasing her employer.

There was a letter waiting for her when she arrived and she opened it excitedly, but her smile slipped away to be replaced by a frown as she read Jess's words. Sitting on a kitchen chair, she placed the letter on the table and stared at it. Her husband's life was at risk, all because of a greedy cleaner at the public house.

Peg was still in the same position when Jim walked through the back door.

'Peg?' he asked, immediately aware that something was wrong.

Picking up the letter, she passed it to him. Once he'd read it, he too took a seat and sighed. 'This confirms it, we have no other choice now.'

Peg merely nodded as Jess's words swirled in her brain. *You could become Kathy's victims of blackmail... she could take every penny you have... Jim is in very great danger...*

'What are we going to do?' Peg asked at last.

'Well, we're not giving her our money should she decide to chance her arm here, that's for sure,' he replied.

'Jim, she could go to the police!'

'Yes, but I don't think she will.'

'Why not?'

'Think about it. She won't be earning much as a cleaner. She's blackmailing Jess for her money which would stop if she goes to the coppers. Also she could be hauled in for harbouring a criminal and face jail time herself.'

'But she ain't. I'm the one harbouring a criminal!'

'Strictly speaking I suppose you are. But remember, she has no proof – it would be her word against mine.'

Jim's words soothed Peg and, realising he was right, she allowed herself to relax a little.

'Now how about some tea because I'm famished,' he said with a smile.

'I've got a bit of brisket,' Peg said, getting to her feet.

'Lovely. I think we should burn that letter, don't you?'

Peg nodded. Jim lit the range and shoved the letter in, watching it burn to ash. Pulling Peg into his arms, he kissed her. 'I love you, Peg Butler, with all my heart and soul.'

'I love you an' all, sweetheart,' she replied, feeling the warmth radiate throughout her body.

As she prepared the meal, she allowed her worries to slip away. Excitedly, she told him about her day in the shop.

Jim listened, murmuring in all the right places but his mind was elsewhere. He was thinking that the threat which was Kathy Frith needed to be removed from their lives – permanently.

* * *

All day, over in Birmingham, the atmosphere had been strained. Kathy was unaware that everyone knew what she was up to and went about her business as usual, her mind on the money she had conned out of Jess. Once her cleaning was finished, Kathy sat in the bar, her eyes on Carter. She scowled as Jess came through after taking her break.

Sipping her gin, Kathy pondered. She would have to wait another week before pay day came round again and Jess's wages became hers. It was a slow but sure way of accumulating funds, but Kathy wanted more. Her mind turned to Jim Butler, the man who had murdered Jess's husband. Maybe it was time he paid for her silence too. In fact, Ellen, Gail and Carter knew of the crime committed so they could pay up as well. Seeing Carter laughing with a customer, Kathy mentally crossed him off her list. She couldn't do that to the man she intended to take as her husband. How that would come about she had no idea as yet, unless... he could wed her in exchange for her keeping her mouth shut. Thrilled at the thought, Kathy's mouth turned up at the corners in an evil little smile.

29

Later that same evening, Kathy told Ellen she was going out and would be back before lock-up.

'I've never known you go out before, are you off to somewhere nice?' Ellen asked.

'The music hall.' Kathy's words sounded like a challenge, almost daring Ellen to refuse her time off, although her cleaning was finished.

'On your own?' Ellen asked.

'Well, I ain't got a man to take me, have I?' Kathy said, casting a glance in Carter's direction.

'I didn't mean anything by it, I was just asking,' Ellen replied meekly, not wishing to send the woman into another rage.

Kathy turned tail and left the kitchen. Going to her room, she collected her bag, went downstairs and out of the pub. As she walked to the theatre, Kathy's mind thrashed out a thought she'd had earlier. She would enjoy the show then wait outside until a certain gentleman came out. She intended to intercept Al Flint on his way home. Once she had his attention, she would explain that Jess Lacey needed to be gone from the pub. Saying Jess's life was in danger, she would elicit Flint's help in removing the thorn in her side.

Arriving at the theatre and happy with her plan, Kathy bought a ticket and went to find a seat.

* * *

Meanwhile, back at the pub, Kathy's outing had sparked a bit of a stir.

'She's never done this before,' Gail said as she served up ham salad with boiled potatoes to the whole team.

'I must admit it made me feel uneasy,' Carter said. 'The way she looked at me gave me the shivers. It was like she was blaming me for her being alone.'

'Her comment was rather pointed,' Ellen agreed.

'She's up to something,' Gail put in.

'Like what?' Jess asked.

'I don't know but I have a feeling we'll find out before too long,' Ellen answered.

Once they had finished their food, Ellen said, 'Carter, get the doors open before the customers riot.'

Jess stood behind the bar while Carter threw open the doors. He was almost knocked off his feet as folk rushed in.

'About bloody time!' a fellow said, pushing past the barman.

'Ellen seems to keep her own hours,' complained another. 'I never know when this place is open or shut!'

'We have to eat, you know,' Carter called out whilst shoving his way through the throng to the counter.

'There ain't enough staff, that's the trouble,' someone else said.

'Quit whining,' Bella instructed as she forced the man aside. 'Two gins, Jess, if you please.'

'Hey, I was afore you!' the man stated.

'You want to make summat of it?' Bella enquired as she towered over him.

'God forbid! Ladies first, I always say.'

Laughter erupted from the crowd as the man stepped aside.

Enid grinned as she took her usual seat.

Paying for the drinks, Bella remarked, 'No Kathy tonight?'

'She's gone to the music hall,' Jess replied.

'By her own self?' Enid asked. Jess nodded and moved to another customer. 'That's strange, ain't it, Bella?'

'Yeah. I wonder what's going on.' Clinking her glass to Enid's, Bella pondered the situation; moreover, she wondered how she could find out what was afoot.

* * *

The evening passed pleasantly enough for Kathy and she took her time leaving the theatre. Not wanting to get caught up in the crush of bodies exiting the building, she also knew it would be a little while before Al Flint came out. He would have to clean off his stage make-up and get changed.

Once outside, Kathy went to hover at the stage door used by the performers. It wasn't unusual for fans to wait here for their favourite acts to emerge, and Kathy just became one of them.

The small crowd chatted as they waited and Kathy stood by herself in the shadows, listening to the conversations. About half an hour later, there was a buzz of excitement as the door opened and the performers filed out into the arms of their adoring public.

'Mr Flint,' Kathy called out as she spied Al come through the door. He turned at hearing his name and Kathy stepped over to him. 'I need to speak with you,' she said.

'Yes – how can I help you?'

'You can get Jess Lacey away from The Queen's Head.' Kathy saw the frown cross his face in the light from the stage-door lamp.

'Who are you?' he asked.

'That ain't important, but what is...'

'Look here, I don't have time for this,' he said, beginning to turn away from the strange woman.

'Jess is in danger, Mr Flint.'

Facing her again, he asked, 'What do you mean?'

'Somebody killed her husband and now they're after her,' Kathy lied.

'Why?' Flint gasped.

'The *why* don't matter. The fact is Jess needs somebody to rescue and protect her.'

'I thought the barman, Carter, would do that, he's clearly in love with her.'

'He ain't!' Kathy snapped. 'I'm Carter's girl. Anyway, I thought you should know. It's up to you what you do about it.' Kathy walked away to disappear into the darkness of a moonless night.

Al Flint stood staring after her with the distinct feeling he'd seen her somewhere before. Walking slowly away from the theatre, he considered the creepy woman's words. Jess Lacey could be at the mercy of a killer but for what reason he had no idea. He wondered if what the stranger had told him was actually true; why would she seek him out and tell him if it were not? The more he thought about it, the more concerned he became. He couldn't stand by and watch Jess be murdered now that he had been made aware of her plight.

Making a decision to visit the pub the following day, Flint strode home. He had to warn Jess that someone was out to kill her. Then, rubbing his chin, he thought, *I must avoid that big Bella as well!*

30

The bar was still busy when Kathy returned to the pub. The music hall had closed at ten o'clock and she had waited around half an hour for Al to come out, then she had walked briskly back to the pub in order to take her usual seat at the end of the counter. Carter served her a gin, asking politely, 'Have you had a nice time?'

'Yeah, it wasn't bad,' she responded, pleased he'd bothered to ask. Sipping her drink, she watching him smiling and joking with the customers. Occasionally her eyes slipped to Jess but almost immediately came back to the man she adored.

Eventually Carter rang the hand bell kept behind the bar and called, 'Time, gentlemen, please!' The patrons groaned loudly, knowing they had to drink up and go home to explain to their wives where the housekeeping money had gone.

After seeing the last man out, Carter shot the bolts on the doors with a huge sigh.

'What a night!' Jess said as she went to the kitchen.

Kathy followed her, lip curled in utter dislike of the girl.

Carter brought up the rear, saying, 'This bar will take some cleaning, it's a real mess.'

'I always do it, don't I?' Kathy snapped.

'Yes, I just meant it's worse than usual,' Carter replied.

Gail provided hot tea and laid out some freshly baked scones. 'Ellen's gone to bed,' she informed the others. 'I'm off as well, leave the cups, I'll see to them in the morning.' After drinking her tea, Jess followed suit.

Carter propped his feet up on a chair to ease the ache in his legs.

'She ain't for you, you know that, don't you?' Kathy said.

Taken aback at the statement, Carter looked at Kathy. 'Jess and I are...'

'No, you ain't!' Kathy's words came out like an order.

'What's got into you?' he asked, taking his feet off the chair.

'If you don't want the coppers round 'ere again you'd best heed my warning.'

'What warning?'

'Stay away from her, Carter, I mean it!'

'Kathy, I don't understand...'

'Then let me spell it out for you. Jess Lacey will be arrested for murdering her husband if you don't marry me.' Carter's mouth fell open in disbelief. 'Remember what I've said because I won't think twice about turning her in to the constabulary.' With that Kathy stood and strode out of the room.

With shock written all over his face, Carter watched her go. It was hours before he was able to turn off the lights and go to his own bed.

* * *

The next morning, Carter refused breakfast and went to the cellar where he could think in peace. He was tired, having had very little sleep the previous night, and still Kathy's words whirled in his mind. He was all in favour of marriage – but to Kathy? Never! However, no matter how much he thought about it he could see no way out. If he wanted to keep Jess safe from the law then he would have to agree to Kathy's terms. He was afraid that Kathy would implicate Jess in Bill's murder, even though she had nothing to do with it. In exchange for her silence, he would have to become her husband. Carter's stomach churned at the very idea.

Meanwhile, up in the bar, Kathy was cleaning like a demon and Jess was restocking the shelves. Ellen and Gail were discussing the idea of providing food for customers.

'What made you think of this?' Ellen asked.

'I overheard someone say they were hungry but didn't want to leave the bar. That was when I wondered if we couldn't provide something like crusty cobs with cheese and pickles. Then in the winter we could make a hot broth and dumplings,' Gail said.

'I like it, we wouldn't have to charge the earth for a simple snack, and I'm sure it will go down well with the punters. Get on to it and we'll see how it goes. Thanks, Gail.'

Jess went to open up as Carter was still in the cellar.

Bella and Enid were amongst the first in, chatting about how slow business had been last night. At their usual table, Enid nudged her friend and tilted her head towards the man walking to the counter. Bella raised an eyebrow and they watched on in silence.

'Jess, may I have a word, please?' the man asked.

'Mr Flint. What can I do for you?'

'I can't say here, it's a private matter and very important.'

Bella and Enid exchanged a glance, curious to know what was going on.

'I can't leave the bar, I'm on my own at present, as you can see.'

'Jess, it's vital I speak with you, it's a matter of life and death!' Flint's harsh whisper had Bella lean forward to better hear the conversation.

'Give me a moment then,' Jess said. She went to the kitchen and told Ellen what Flint had said.

'Right, bring him through here and I'll get Carter on the bar,' Ellen said.

Once in the kitchen, Jess asked, 'What is it, Mr Flint?'

Looking around at Gail and Ellen, he took a breath then said, 'Last night as I left the theatre a woman approached me saying your husband had been killed and you were next.'

Jess gasped and dropped onto a chair.

'Who was this harbinger of doom?' Ellen asked.

'She wouldn't say but she called you by name, Jess, and I was worried stiff...'

'Thank you, Mr Flint, for your concern and for sharing this information,' Ellen said. 'I can assure you Jess is in no danger here.'

'Maybe not, but what about when she leaves the pub?'

'We'll ensure she's safe at all times,' Gail added.

'I was told to get her away from here,' Al pressed on.

'Excuse me, but I am in the room!' Jess snapped, bringing Ellen and Al's attention to her. 'I apologise, I didn't mean to shout. Thank you, Mr Flint, I think I know what all this is about. I will deal with it so please don't concern yourself further.'

With a nod, Al Flint got to his feet and left via the back door. He'd done everything he could to ensure Jess's safety. Now it was up to her friends to shield her from harm, he could do no more.

A sense of relief washed over him as he strode home at having passed the burden on to someone else. He also resolved not to go to the pub again, it was dangerous and he didn't want to be involved any further.

'Well, we all know now how Kathy spent her time last evening,' Ellen said, raising her eyes to the ceiling.

Upstairs, Kathy was busy cleaning, blissfully unaware that she'd been rumbled yet again.

31

Peg Butler was very happy in her job at Amelia's and business was brisk. However, always in the back of her mind was Jess's letter warning her about Kathy Frith. Although the cleaner had made no contact as yet, it didn't mean that she wouldn't in the future, and Peg worried about it constantly. She and Jim had not discussed the matter since the letter had been burned, but Peg knew she would have to broach the subject again soon if only to ease her own mind.

Checking the rails of garments to ensure they were all priced up, Peg heard Jim's voice in her mind again – *we have no other choice now.* She knew exactly what he'd meant by that and she fretted he might try to act on it. The last thing she needed to hear was that Kathy Frith had turned up dead.

Shaking off the thoughts, Peg plastered a smile on her face as she greeted a customer.

* * *

Over on the building site, Jim, Harry, Bert and George sat on upturned buckets to eat their mid-morning sandwich and drink their tea.

'Have you heard anything from that cleaner yet, Jim?' Harry asked.

'No, mate, and I tell you, it's got me worried.'

'What're we gonna do about it then?' Bert asked, spitting crumbs everywhere.

Jim shook his head. 'I ain't got a clue.'

'I don't like it – the sword of Damocles hanging over your head,' George added.

'Blimey, hark at him!' Harry said with a grin.

'He's right though, Harry, it's putting a strain on me and Peg. Every day when I go home I expect to find Peg in tears 'cos that woman has visited with another threat.'

'Summat has to be done, you know that, right?' Bert said quietly.

'This Kathy has everyone dancing to her tune and before long somebody will get tired of it,' George said.

'That somebody is me, fellas. It's time to get this sorted out once and for all,' Jim stated.

'We are with you, pal, just give us the nod.' The others mumbled their agreement at Harry's words.

Jim's tight-lipped smile by way of thanks prompted them to clink their chipped mugs together in a show of camaraderie.

Jim pondered the situation all day as he laid rows of bricks but by knocking-off time he was none the wiser. He walked home, not having reached a conclusion to the dilemma facing him. He knew that to keep himself and his friends out of jail he would have to silence Kathy Frith permanently. However, the thought of killing her turned his stomach. He wasn't sure he could do it despite the gravity of the situation. Yes, he had murdered Bill Lacey in cold blood because of the beating the man had given Peg, but disposing of the cleaner was a different matter entirely. As yet the woman had done nothing to either him or Peg. Could he justify taking her life on the off-chance she would talk and have him arrested? He didn't think so. Then again, if he was hauled in, taken to court and found guilty – he could hang. The thought of dancing on the end of a rope made him shiver but also reach a decision. He couldn't put it off any longer – he had to discuss it in detail with Peg.

Once they had finished their evening meal, Peg and Jim sat in the living room. 'What's on your mind, sweet'eart? Or can I guess?' Peg asked. Jim had been quiet since he arrived home from work and she was concerned.

'I've been thinking about Jess's letter,' he answered.

'And?' she prompted.

'I'm bothered by it, darlin', I can't lie.'

'Well, we ain't had a visit or a blackmail letter from that woman...' Peg began.

'True, but we could yet. She could get me hung, Peg.'

'Dear God!' Peg's hand flew to her mouth. 'This is all my fault. If I had told Bill where Jess was in the first place, he wouldn't have beaten me and you wouldn't have had to...' Peg let the sentence hang in mid-air.

'You would never have told on your friend if you didn't have to, Peg, we both know that. It's not your fault, it's Bill's. He was the one who started all this by belting Jess!'

'I know you're right but what can we do?'

'Put your glad rags on, petal, I'm taking you to visit Jess.'

'Ooh, Jim! Hang on, the cleaner will be there.'

'We'll have a nice private conversation with Jess and see where we go from there.'

* * *

Unaware that her friends were on their way to see her, Jess was in the office with Ellen, discussing Al Flint's visit. Carter was tending the bar, Kathy was drinking and Gail was cooking.

'This is getting ridiculous, Ellen!' Jess exclaimed. 'Maybe I should move out and then Kathy will be happy.'

'Will she though? Jess, she wants Carter and you leaving won't change that; he'll be distraught if you go. Besides, Kathy will still have the upper hand because she knows our secret.'

Jess paced the room, wringing her hands. 'There must be something we can do!'

'I don't see what. She has us all over a barrel, I'm afraid.'

'Well, I'm not paying her another penny, Ellen!'

'Jess, be careful, she could have your friend, Jim, swinging on the gallows.'

Dropping onto a chair, Jess nodded, all the fight knocked out of her. 'I'd best get back to work.'

Leaving the office, Jess took over the bar from Carter who immediately went to see Ellen.

'It's busy in here today,' she said as Carter closed the door.

'Ellen, Kathy will have Jess arrested for killing her husband if I don't wed her!'

'But Jess didn't kill him!' Ellen said.

'You and I know that, but Kathy could implicate Jess somehow saying she was in on it. I'm worried, Ellen, very worried!'

Ellen groaned and rubbed her forehead. 'This is going from bad to worse. First blackmailing Jess for money, then Flint's visit and now bribing you to marry her.'

'I can't do it, Ellen!' Carter shivered, running his hands down his arms as if brushing away something nasty. 'I can't be tied to her for the rest of my life!'

'You won't have to be. We'll come up with something. Just... try and be as normal as you can and give me some time to think about it.'

'Don't take too long, please, I don't want that woman dragging me down the aisle, and me not able to do anything about it.'

Ellen nodded and Carter went back to work.

Sitting at the bar, Kathy almost choked on her gin when she saw Jim walk in with a lady on his arm.

'Jess!' Peg called out.

'Peg! How lovely to see you!' The two women hugged over the counter as Carter and Jim shook hands.

Quite the little reunion, Kathy thought as she watched from her perch. She couldn't hear what was being said because of the noise in the bar. She frowned when Carter went through to the kitchen and came back a moment later with Ellen.

Kathy clenched her teeth hard enough to break them when a little later Jess, Peg, Jim and Carter all left the pub together. *What the hell is going on?*

Ellen took over serving and Kathy called for another gin. 'Where have they gone?' she asked.

'I've given them some time off to be with their friends,' Ellen replied.

'You don't give me time off,' Kathy said. 'Except that one time when I went to the music hall.'

'That's because you have no friends,' Ellen replied before stepping away to pull a pint for a customer. She was fast running out of patience with the girl, and even at the risk of upsetting her again, Ellen was finding it hard to hold her tongue.

Kathy gave her employer a look that could crisp bacon before sipping her drink.

Bella and Enid guffawed loudly at Ellen's remark before resuming their conversation about how nice it was that Jess was spending time with her friends.

32

Not far away in a coffee shop, Jess, Carter, Jim and Peg sat at a table in a quiet corner.

'We've come to talk about what's to be done about Kathy,' Jim said.

'I have something to tell you first,' Carter said. Relating the ultimatum given to him by the cleaner, he then went on, 'I'm sorry, Jess, I couldn't find a chance to tell you before.'

'You can't marry her, Carter!' Jess gushed.

'I won't. Ellen's thinking about what we can do to get out of this mess.'

'As we all have been,' Jim said. 'I think I know what you'll say but we can't let this go on any longer. Kathy's getting bolder and God only knows what she'll come up with next.'

'Jess, Jim could hang if that woman opens her mouth,' Peg said quietly.

'I know, but how can we solve this? I don't want to hand her my wages every week, and I certainly won't stand by and see her marry Carter!'

Patting Jess's arm, Carter whispered, 'Calm down, my love, that's not going to happen.'

'The boys are with us if we decide to…' Jim faltered, unable to finish the sentence.

None of them spoke, each considering the ramifications of the unspoken idea.

'Can I get you anything more?' The waitress came over, breaking the silence.

'Not unless you serve alcohol,' Carter said.

'I'm afraid not, sir, sorry.' With a smile, the waitress wandered away.

'We should set Bella onto her,' Carter said with a wry grin.

'The big lady?' Jim asked.

'That's the one, she laid out a punter with one punch.'

'Bloody hell!' Jim exclaimed.

'I wonder if she would know someone who could deal with our little problem,' Jess muttered as if to herself.

'It's best we don't involve anyone else, Jess, the secret must be kept at all costs,' Carter said.

'Of course. Sorry, I was just thinking aloud.' However, that germ of an idea took root and began to grow, and no matter how hard she tried, Jess could not forget it.

No further on in finding a solution to the Kathy problem, Peg and Jim caught the train back to Wednesbury and Jess and Carter walked back to the pub arm in arm.

'It was lovely to see Peg and Jim, even though we didn't come up with a plan,' Jess confessed.

'The whole thing is such a mess, and I'm tempted to leave it with Jim and his friends.'

'Carter, we can't!'

Sighing loudly, Carter went on. 'I know, but we're going

round in circles getting nowhere fast, and all the time Kathy is laughing at us.'

Entering the pub via the back door, they were greeted by Gail. 'Any luck?' she enquired.

Jess shook her head then whispered what she'd been told by Carter.

'Marry – you and Kathy in exchange for her keeping quiet?' Gail aimed her question at Carter. When he nodded, she went on, 'I hope you told her no!'

'She didn't give me a chance,' Carter said feebly. 'If I refuse, she'll go to the coppers.'

Gail blew out her cheeks then Jess said, 'We should get to work, Ellen will need a break.' Jess and Carter took over the running of the bar and a grateful Ellen went to put her feet up in the kitchen.

Kathy watched avidly from her seat. Carter was not his usual jovial self and she wondered why. Clearly their little outing had not been much of a success as evidenced by his long face.

Eventually Carter persuaded the last customer to leave and then he locked up.

'You don't look happy,' Kathy said to him after Jess went to the kitchen.

'I'm all right,' he responded.

'Have you thought on what I said?'

'Yes, I have.'

'And?'

'I can't wed you, Kathy.'

With a look which would have made the thunder god proud, she yelled, 'Why not?'

'Because I don't love you. I love Jess.'

Kathy's scream was loud enough to shatter glass and brought the others running in from the kitchen.

'What's going on?' Ellen asked.

'I've told her I won't marry her because I'm in love with Jess,' Carter said.

Kathy's legs gave way and she crumpled to the floor, sobbing loudly.

'Kathy love, let's get you to bed.' Ellen took a step but stopped when Kathy's arm shot out.

'Stay away from me!' she screeched.

'Kathy...' Jess began.

'You shut your mouth, you whore!' Kathy rasped.

Everyone was shocked at the cleaner's outburst but no one moved.

Getting to her feet, Kathy's eyes burned with hatred at Jess. 'You think you've won, don't yer? Well, you ain't 'cos tomorrer I'm off to the cop shop to tell 'em all about how your friend Jim killed yer husband.'

The colour drained from Jess's face and she stumbled against Gail, who held her up.

'There's no need...' Ellen said.

'Oh, there's every need!' Kathy spat. Pointing to Carter, she went on. 'He should be marrying me!' Then to Jess she said, 'You could never make him happy like I can.'

'That's the gin talking.' Ellen tried to calm the cleaner down.

'No, it ain't. I want money from you all and Carter's ring on my finger or else I tell the bobbies everything.'

'Please, Kathy...' Jess begged.

In one swift motion, Kathy grabbed an empty glass from a nearby table and launched it at Jess. It struck her just above her left eyebrow before crashing to the floor. Jess staggered back, her hand going instinctively to the injury.

'Kathy! Stop this right now!' Carter yelled.

Looking at him, Kathy lowered her eyes subserviently.

Gail was fussing over Jess and Ellen breathed a sigh of relief that Carter appeared to have the situation under control.

That relief, however, was short lived.

33

A moment later, another dirty glass flew across the room, chasing the other women back towards the kitchen.

'Kathy love,' Carter cooed, 'calm down, sweetheart.' He held his hands out as he tentatively stepped towards the raging woman.

'No!'

'I don't like to see you like this, petal.' Carter was doing his best to defuse the situation.

'You said you d'aint love me,' Kathy murmured as she reached out for another glass on the table.

'I know.' Carter edged closer as he spoke. 'I think I may have been wrong about that.'

'So you do?'

'Put down the glass, darlin', and come to me,' he coaxed, holding out his arms for Kathy to walk into.

Dropping the glass, Kathy ran to be enveloped by Carter's strong arms. She cried softly as he held her and stroked her hair.

'There, that's much better, isn't it?' he asked. He felt her nod against his chest but his eyes were on the others as they crept back into the bar.

'Come on, let's get you to bed,' Carter said quietly. Kathy looked up at him with soulful eyes and he smiled. 'No, no hanky-panky. I believe a maiden should be just that until she's wed.'

With a nod, Kathy allowed herself to be led out of the bar, the others having moved out of the way. At the stairs, she stood on tiptoe and kissed Carter's cheek. 'Goodnight, sweetheart.'

'Sleep well, Kathy,' he responded.

Once they were sure she'd gone, Ellen checked Jess's forehead. A lump was beginning to form but otherwise she was unharmed. 'You'll have a nasty bruise there and a headache,' Gail said, wetting a towel and giving it to Jess to hold in place.

'Bloody hellfire and damnation!' Ellen cussed. 'I can't believe what I've just witnessed.'

'Summat ain't right in that girl's head,' Gail added.

'Well, this cannot go on!' Ellen stated. 'She's added injury to insult now and something *has* to be done about it!'

'Let's all calm down and try to think clearly,' Carter suggested.

'I'll make some tea,' Gail proffered.

'Good idea, then we can discuss this rationally,' Carter said.

And so they did, long into the night until eventually they went to bed, all feeling thoroughly exhausted.

* * *

The following day, Kathy behaved as though nothing had happened. Cleaning up the broken glass in the bar, she muttered about people being careless, seemingly unaware that she had been the one to shatter it. She then went outside to wash the windows, sniffing loudly as Bella and Enid walked in.

'What happened to you?' Bella demanded to know as she spied the lump on Jess's forehead.

Jess quickly explained the events of the previous night.

'What set her off?' Bella asked.

'I can't tell you,' Jess answered.

'Can't or won't?'

'Bella, my friend is in trouble and Kathy is threatening to tell the police. That's all I can say.' Jess had whispered the brief explanation so as not to be overheard.

'She needs to be got rid of,' Bella said out of the corner of her mouth. 'I can help you there if you want. I know a man.' With a wink, Bella took the drinks to where Enid was waiting.

'What was all that about?' Enid asked.

'Do you know if Four Fingers Fred is still around?' Bella answered with a question of her own.

'Ar, he's living over the back of the police station in Digbeth – why?'

'I was just wondering.'

'Bella Jervis, you don't never *just wonder* about anything, so tell me.'

'You have to keep your gob shut then.' Assured Enid wouldn't say a word to a soul, Bella revealed what she had heard from Jess.

'I wonder what the trouble is,' Enid said.

'I don't know but it must be big. Anyway, I said I knew a man who could help,' Bella replied.

'Four Fingers Fred,' Enid said as the penny dropped.

'Precisely. He's got some nerve living by the constabulary, especially in his line of work.'

'Hiding in plain sight,' Enid said with a little laugh. Then in a whisper added, 'I don't think he's offed anybody in a while though.'

'Maybe not, but he won't have forgotten how, it would be like riding a bike to him.'

The two women laughed and sipped their gins.

Bella's words rolled around in Jess's mind – *I know a man*. She wondered how much it would cost, then she shuddered. Was she really considering hiring a man to murder Kathy? Pushing the thoughts aside, she concentrated on her work.

Inevitably, all day Jess was asked about the lump on her forehead so she explained it away by saying she'd collided with an open cupboard door. She wasn't sure if she was believed but none of the customers pushed for any more information, much to her relief.

Ordering more drinks, Bella asked, 'Do you want me to contact my man?'

'No, Bella, but thank you,' Jess replied.

With a curt nod, Bella returned to her seat.

'I know they call Fred Four Fingers because he's missing his pinky on his left hand, but I don't know how he lost it,' Enid said.

'The story goes that he used to work for a gangster called Teddy D'Veen. Now this D'Veen was into all sorts; he had rackets going on all over the place. Thieving on a grand scale, like that time a shipment of fur coats went missing. Then the gold quarter workshops were broken into and the jewellery was pinched.'

'Ar, I remember that,' Enid interrupted.

'There were folk who disappeared an' all, some turned up floating in the cut, others were never seen again.'

'Courtesy of D'Veen?' Enid asked.

Bella nodded. 'Fred Marvin was a collector for D'Veen; he

collected the money from the businesses in exchange for protection. As I understand it, Fred's wife had ideas above her station and wanted to live the high life. So, Fred started to skim a bit off the takings each week. Eventually D'Veen noticed that Fred's money was lighter than the others.'

'I bet D'Veen was angry,' Enid said.

'He sure was. One day D'Veen called Fred into his office to explain the missing funds.'

'Did he confess?'

'Yeah, after a little encouragement,' Bella said, raising her eyebrows. 'D'Veen had him beaten, then as compensation he took Fred's little finger.'

'It's a strange thing to do though.'

'D'Veen said because Fred had been light-fingered with his money, he could be for real.'

'Oh, I see now.'

'Then he became known as Four Fingers Fred. Naturally, he behaved himself after that.'

'What happened to D'Veen?' Enid asked.

'Apparently he went to the Americas where it's said racketeering is rife.'

'The coppers would have been glad to see the back of him.'

'I expect so, but Four Fingers Fred was for sure. He has his own little gang now but sensibly he keeps it low key.'

'Bribing the constabulary to look the other way,' End said.

'Without a doubt,' Bella agreed. 'Let's have another gin before we go to work 'cos it's getting late and we'll miss all the decent punters.'

Enid thought about the tale she'd just heard and subconsciously tucked her little finger into a fist.

34

That evening, from her perch at the end of the bar, Kathy watched Carter adoringly. He had held her lovingly the previous night and Kathy smiled inwardly at the memory. It was proof he preferred her over Jess and Kathy was thrilled about it. Nevertheless, Jess Lacey was still here and so the threat remained; Kathy knew Jess could take him away from her.

At first the blackmail had been all about the money she could acquire for keeping silent, and although it was still important, now Carter was her priority. He had finally shown that he cared for her by wrapping his arms around her in front of everyone. Now Kathy was intent on ensuring Carter Adams continued to be her man.

Gin in hand, Kathy began to fantasise about marrying Carter. He would book the church and get a new suit, and of course she would need a gown. Once the ceremony was over, they would return to the pub and she would move into his room with him. There she would give herself to him, body, heart and soul. He would be hers until death parted them.

A smile spread across her lips as Carter took her glass to refill it.

'Thanks, sweetheart,' Kathy called out, enjoying the looks from nearby drinkers. 'That's my fella, that is.'

Carter winced as he placed the glass on the counter. He couldn't deny it for fear of Kathy causing a scene.

Jess quietly fumed but could do nothing either.

'Ain't you gonna congratulate me?' Kathy went on.

'What for?' one of the punters asked.

'Carter and me – we'm to be wed.'

All around them, glasses were raised in a salute and Carter cringed. Coming to stand next to him, Jess whispered, 'She's gone too far now!'

'Ignore her, Jess, we'll sort it out later after lock-up.'

Jess stepped away, furious with the cleaner who was drunkenly announcing her supposed wedding to all and sundry. Unable to hide her anger, Jess stamped into the kitchen where Gail and Ellen were having tea.

'That bloody woman!' Jess cursed.

'What's she done now?' Ellen asked.

'She's told everyone that she and Carter are betrothed!'

'What?' Gail was nonplussed at Kathy's audacity.

'I can't do this any more, I'm going to have to leave,' Jess said, a lone tear running down her cheek.

'No, you're not,' Ellen said. 'Wait 'til we're closed then we'll thrash it out with Kathy.'

'She's drunk again, and you know what will happen if we upset her,' Jess pointed to the lump on her forehead. 'Next time she could have my eye out!'

'You stay in here with Gail, have a cuppa and I'll go and help Carter in the bar.' Ellen got to her feet and, giving Jess a quick hug, she left the kitchen.

'Bella said she knows a man who could...' Jess began as she accepted the tea offered.

'You haven't told her what's been going on!'

'No. I just said I had a friend in trouble.'

'It's looking like it's coming to that though,' Gail said quietly.

'Gail, I don't know what to do! I'm so miserable.'

'I can see that, and I can't do anything to help you feel better, though I wish I could.'

The friends sat in silence, listening to the noise coming from the bar. When someone began to whistle the wedding march, Jess burst into tears.

By the time Carter locked up later that evening, Jess was exhausted from crying.

Kathy swayed her way into the kitchen with a wide grin. She sat at the table and, seeing Jess's tear-stained face, asked, 'What's up with you?'

Anger instantly bubbled to the surface and Jess rounded on her. 'How dare you announce to the world that you and Carter are to be married!'

'And why shouldn't I?'

'Because it's not true!' Jess boomed.

'Ah, but it is, because if he don't wed me then your little pal goes to the gallows.'

Jess jumped out of her chair, all set to attack, but Carter caught her and held her back.

Kathy was too drunk even to flinch. She burst out laughing then said, 'You'm in the shit up to your eyeballs, Jess Lacey, and well you know it.'

Ellen and Gail stood by, horrified at what was taking place.

Jess struggled to be free of Carter's arms, intent on causing injury to Kathy.

'Stop it!' Ellen shouted. 'Get to bed, all of you!'

Once she was released, Jess sulkily obeyed the order. Carter followed behind and Gail said, 'I'll help Kathy, she's in no fit state to manage the stairs.' Ellen nodded. 'Come on, time for sleep,' Gail encouraged Kathy to stand.

Ellen rested her elbows on the table, her head in her hands, groaning at how dysfunctional her little family had become.

Gail managed to get Kathy through the doorway, saying, 'You can be such a bitch at times.'

'I know,' Kathy replied with a laugh.

'Why are you doing this to Jess?'

'Because… I hate her! She tried to steal Carter away from me, but it d'aint work, did it?'

'He won't marry you,' Gail said as they stopped at the bottom of the stairs.

Looking directly into Gail's eyes, Kathy replied, 'Oh, he will, if he knows what's good for him.'

'Come on, let's get you to bed,' Gail said but her mind was racing. How could she help sort this whole mess out? As she pushed Kathy from behind, taking one step at a time, an idea began to form in her mind. Could she do it? She knew she would have to, it was the only way.

At the top of the stairs, Gail whispered in Kathy's ear, 'You've gone too far now so this is for Jess.' Spinning the drunken woman around, Gail pushed her hard, greedily watching the cleaner bounce on every step to the bottom.

Ellen heard the scream and came running. She found Kathy on the floor at the bottom of the stairs, her head at a peculiar angle. Clearly the cleaner was dead. 'Oh my God!' she gasped. Looking at Gail, she asked, 'What happened?' shock written all over her face.

Jess and Carter came rushing from their rooms to see what the noise was about.

Ellen looked up at Gail, who said simply, 'She fell.'

35

'Oh my God! What are we to do?' Ellen asked as she gazed at the body.

'Don't touch her,' Carter advised. 'We'll need the doctor.'

'I'll go,' Gail said as she came down the stairs, carefully stepping around Kathy. She dashed from the pub via the back door.

'What happened?' Jess asked, finally finding her tongue.

'Well, Gail said she fell,' Ellen replied with a hand on her forehead.

'Did Kathy fall or was she pushed?' Carter asked.

'Gail would never... would she?' Jess asked, staring at the lifeless form.

'Shouldn't we cover her up or something?' Ellen asked.

'No, leave everything as it is for the doctor to see. He will advise us when he gets here.'

Jess and Ellen nodded at Carter's wise words.

It took half an hour for Gail to return with Dr Philpott. 'What do we have here then?' he asked as he spied the body.

'Kathy, our cleaner...' Ellen began.

'She was very drunk, doctor,' Carter put in.

With a nod, the doctor bent down. 'I can smell the alcohol from here,' he said. He checked for a pulse and finding none he shook his head. Standing again, he looked at her head then up the stairs. 'This lady's death is consistent with a fall down the stairs, I would say, resulting in her neck being broken.'

Jess's eyes found Gail's but she saw no guilt there. Perhaps Kathy really had fallen after all.

Dr Philpott wrote out a death certificate and handed it to Ellen.

'Do we need to notify the police?' Ellen asked.

'I don't think that will be necessary,' Dr Philpott answered confidently.

'I managed to get her to the top of the stairs but it was when I went to open her bedroom door that I heard her scream,' Gail explained. 'I was too far away to prevent her stumbling.'

'With all that alcohol in her system, I'm surprised she made it as far as she did. She would have been very unsteady on her feet,' the doctor said. 'Her death was clearly accidental.'

Carter paid the doctor and saw him out with their thanks.

'Now what do we do?' Jess asked, the shock finally beginning to wear off.

'I'll fetch the undertaker,' Carter said. 'You girls go to the kitchen and have some tea; it will calm your nerves. There's nothing more to be done here.'

Ready to obey his instruction, they watched him go to knock up the undertaker.

Once Gail had made the tea and they'd all sat down with a cup, Ellen asked, 'Gail, did Kathy really fall?'

'Yes, I told you,' Gail lied.

'The poor woman,' Jess whispered.

'What? You feel sorry for her after what she's done to you?' Gail snapped.

'It's not a nice way to die,' Jess said.

'No way to die is nice, Jess, but God knows she had it coming!'

'Gail...?'

'No, Jess, I didn't do it. She fell, even Dr Philpott said it. How could you even think...?'

'I'm sorry,' Jess interrupted. 'I don't know what I was thinking. Please forgive me.'

Gail nodded and quiet descended as they awaited Carter and the undertaker.

A while later, the clip-clop of horses' hooves alerted the women to the arrival of the undertaker's wagon pulling into the yard. Carter led two men dressed in black into the kitchen.

'Mr Webb at your service,' one said, tipping his top hat.

'Thank you for coming so quickly,' Ellen said.

'This way, Mr Webb,' Carter said, showing the funeral director through to where Kathy's crumpled body lay.

'Thank you, sir, you can leave it with us now,' Mr Webb said. Going out to the cart, Mr Webb and his assistant carried in a coffin. Carefully, they lifted Kathy into it and placed the lid on top. Then the box was taken to the cart.

Mr Webb returned to the kitchen where he suggested someone visit his parlour to choose a funeral package. 'I'll come tomorrow,' Ellen assured him.

Tipping his hat once more, he bade them goodnight. Carter went out to close the yard gates then came back to a silent kitchen.

Jess poured tea for him as they all looked at each other. No one knew what to say. Suddenly a pounding on the front door made them all jump.

'Oh, God, now what?' Ellen rasped.

'I'll go,' Carter said.

The women heard voices and were surprised to see Bella and Enid following Carter.

'What's occurred?' Bella asked. 'We saw Webb's wagon leaving.'

Carter explained everything: Kathy broadcasting she was to marry him, and how when very drunk she had fallen down the stairs and broken her neck.

'Good grief!' Enid exclaimed.

'Well, Kathy can't tell the coppers nothing now, can she?' Bella asked.

All eyes turned to Jess. 'I mentioned that my friend was in trouble and Kathy was going to go to the police. That's all I said.'

'That's true,' Bella confirmed.

'So, you won't be needing Four Fingers Fred after all then?' Enid asked innocently.

Bella rolled her eyes and one by one each face began to smile. The tension of the last few weeks was broken and they all felt they could breathe easier.

After having a hot drink, Bella and Enid went back to work and Jess said, 'I must let Peg and Jim know what's happened.'

'Why don't you and Gail go over tomorrow morning and visit Peg?' Ellen suggested.

'She'll be at work in Amelia's shop.'

'Then go and buy a new frock while you're there. Make a special day of it.' Jess nodded her thanks. 'We'll close tomorrow, I'll put a notice up saying we're shut due to a bereavement.'

'I'll see to the draymen while you go to Webb's then,' Carter said.

'I feel so relieved Kathy can't hurt us any more, but I can't help but feel guilty,' Jess said quietly.

'Well, don't because this is a new start for you,' Gail replied.

'Let's get to bed, tomorrow is another day,' Ellen suggested.

In her room, Gail looked at herself in the mirror. 'Now I have another secret to keep,' she whispered.

36

The next morning, Ellen pinned a notice on the door of the pub and set off for the funeral parlour. Carter shifted empty barrels to make room for the full ones to be delivered later while Jess and Gail walked across town to the railway station.

'Jess?'

Hearing her name called, Jess turned to see Al Flint. 'Mr Flint, how are you?'

'I'm well, and very glad to see you are too. I've been worried about you.'

'As you see, I'm fine. You remember Gail, I'm sure,' Jess said, turning to her friend.

'I do. Nice to see you. Off somewhere nice, are we?' Flint asked.

'Dress shopping and visiting a friend,' Jess confirmed.

'I'll not keep you then.' Flint bowed his head to each girl before turning on his heel and marching away. As he went, he breathed a sigh of relief that Jess had not been harmed in any way.

'That's the first time we've seen him since he came to the pub all doom and gloom,' Gail said.

'Yes, and I doubt we'll be seeing any more of him,' Jess replied.

'With luck. I just couldn't take to the man, I don't know why,' Gail said as they continued towards the station.

'It seems wrong to be going to buy new clothes when Kathy is...' Jess began.

'Life goes on, Jess. You can't not do things because someone has died.'

'You're right, I know, but...'

'I tell you what, we'll go first class and have coffee and cake on the train,' Gail suggested.

Purchasing their tickets, the pair strode out onto the platform. As many women on the way to buy new dresses will do, they checked out the clothes of the other passengers waiting patiently.

'I like that black and red over there,' Gail said, tilting her head in the direction of a lady on the arm of a gentleman. The red dress with its long sleeves was fitted around the lady's tiny waist. Lying over a small bustle at the back, it fell to her ankles. It was trimmed with black braid and buttons in the Zouave style, the name of which was taken from the Algerian Zouave troops who fought in the 1859 Italian war.

'So do I,' Jess concurred.

A screaming child drew their attention to a woman whose clothes were no better than rags. A badly patched skirt over worn-out boots and a none-too-clean blouse with mismatched buttons was clearly the woman's Sunday best attire.

'Quite a difference between them, isn't there?' Jess said.

'Yeah, that's what money does for you,' Gail replied.

The chug of the steam engine crawling into the station

prompted everyone on the platform to step back a pace. As the train drew to a halt, the porters hurried to open the doors for passengers to alight. Gail and Jess walked to the first carriages and climbed aboard. 'This is very decadent,' Jess said.

'Ain't it just.'

The girls looked around at the rich blue velvet padded seats, small mahogany tables with a mirror shine, and delicate gas lamps cleverly hanging from the ceiling. The large window afforded them a marvellous view, as well as allowing others to see into what they were missing by travelling second or third class.

Settling into a seat with a table, they were approached by an attendant. 'Can I get you anything, ladies?'

'Coffee and cake for two, please,' Gail answered.

The steward nodded and hurried away. In a matter of moments, a trolley was wheeled their way. A two-tiered stand full of cakes was placed on the table along with china cups and saucers, plates, sugar bowl and milk jug, as well as a silver pot of coffee, linen napkins and the bill.

'Thank you,' Jess said.

'Enjoy,' the steward replied before pushing his trolley away to serve someone else.

Gail poured the coffee as the train doors were slammed shut by the porters. The guards blew their whistles and the train began to move.

'Ooh, the coffee is really hot, just the way I like it,' Gail said.

'This is lovely, I think I'll always travel this way in the future,' Jess said, helping herself to a little cake with icing on the top.

'You'll soon run out of money if you do,' Gail advised with a big smile as she chose a slice of chocolate cake.

'Then let's take pleasure in it while we can.'

'Of course we have a first-class return too,' Gail reminded her friend.

Enjoying the refreshments, the girls looked out of the window as they sped past houses and factories, scrubland and yet more dwellings.

The steward appeared once more to clear the table and Jess paid the bill with her thanks. All too soon, the engine slowed and chugged into the station where the girls alighted. They decided to walk to the clothes shop as the weather was still quite clement and they had all the time in the world.

When Jess and Gail entered the premises, Peg rushed to her friend and gave her a hug. 'Jess, how lovely to see you! What a wonderful surprise!'

Peg introduced Jess and Gail to Amelia and then they explained they were there to purchase new attire. Amelia and Gail perused the rails while Peg and Jess chose a dress and went into the fitting room.

'I had to come and tell you,' Jess whispered, 'Kathy is dead.'

'What? How?' Peg was aghast.

'She was blind drunk and fell down the stairs and broke her neck.'

'Crikey!' Peg could hardly believe her ears. Jess told her friend the details of the unfortunate demise of the cleaner as she tried on the chosen dress. 'Thank God! I mean only that Jim is safe at last,' Peg said.

'No more worries on that score,' Jess agreed.

'What will folk think about you and Carter stepping out together after Kathy was trumpeting to all and sundry that he was to wed her?'

'I don't know, Peg. All I can hope is he explains that Kathy was under a misapprehension due to her not being right in the head,' Jess said.

'Time will tell but at least we can rest easier in our beds. Now, how do you like the frock?'

'Truth be told, I don't much. Can we find something else? I saw a lovely red and black one on a lady at the station.' Jess described the outfit as best as she could remember.

'Of course. Take that one off and I'll have another look,' Peg said. Moments later, Peg came back with a similar design to the red one Jess had described but in black and white.

'Oh, yes!' Jess said. 'That's more like it.' When it fit like a glove, Jess asked Peg to box it.

'It's expensive,' Peg warned.

'I don't care. I rarely buy myself anything. I deserve a treat.'

Back in the shop area, Peg boxed the garment and Jess handed over her payment. Gail, in the meantime, had chosen a burgundy Merino wool jacket and skirt, ideal for autumn and winter wear.

As the friends prepared to leave, Peg said, 'Jim will be pleased to know of your visit.'

'We'll meet up again soon,' Jess replied with a smile. 'It's so good to see you doing so well. I'm really happy for you.'

Once they'd said their goodbyes, Jess and Gail strolled to the railway station, chatting about their new purchases. Jess decided to share her worries about what Peg had said regarding people believing Kathy's claims that she would be marrying Carter.

'It shouldn't be a problem,' Gail assured her. 'Everyone knew Kathy wasn't right in the head.'

'I hope you're right. Gossip can be ruinous.'

As they waited on the platform, Jess couldn't help but worry that she and Carter could very well be ostracised once it was known they were an item.

37

Jim Butler listened as his wife told him all about Jess's visit and what she'd learned about the blackmailing cleaner.

'So, this Gail took her upstairs?' he asked when Peg had finished.

'Apparently.'

'Jess and Gail are good friends?'

'Yes, why? Blimey, you don't think…?' Peg gasped.

'It's a thought, love. Maybe Gail had also had enough of Kathy's nonsense and to protect Jess she…'

'Pushed Kathy down the stairs!' Peg finished his sentence.

'Did the police attend?' Jim asked after a moment.

'No, just the doctor.'

'Ah, well, then everyone is in the clear so no need for us to speculate further.'

'I'm so relieved, Jim, I've been so scared you'd be found out and hauled off to the nick.'

'Well, it sounds like nobody is going to jail, sweetheart, so you can stop fretting.' Jim wrapped his wife in his arms and kissed her hair. 'Hmm, you smell lovely,' he murmured.

'Hey, none of that, I have to cook the tea.'

'To hell with tea.' Jim scooped a giggling Peg off her feet and carried her upstairs to their bedroom. Tea was very late that evening.

* * *

The following day, the pub opened as usual and people crowded into the bar, wanting to know who had died. Once the customers heard that Kathy had passed away, condolences were offered to Carter for the loss of his betrothed.

When he'd been offered commiserations for the dozenth time, Carter had had enough and rang the hand bell, calling for everyone's attention. 'I need to make it clear that Kathy and I were not to be wed. She was poorly in the head and it was all a delusion.'

'So she believed it but it weren't true?' The question fired at Carter came from a man at the back of the room.

'Exactly. I'm sure some of you will already know, but for those who don't – Jess and I have been walking out for a while now.'

Whistles and applause filled the bar and Jess thought, *what was it the ancient Roman senators used to say? Ah, yes – the mob is fickle. One minute they feel sorry for you and the next they're cheering you on.*

Whilst Carter and Jess manned the bar, Ellen and Gail went to clear Kathy's room. 'She didn't have much,' Ellen said.

'You think?' Gail had opened the top drawer in the dresser. 'Look at this.'

Ellen did as she was bid and gasped. She lifted out the money which had been thrown there.

'How did she get all this?' Gail asked.

'She had Jess's wages but it was a pittance compared to...'

'How much is there?'

Ellen began to count and eventually she said, 'Ten pounds.'

Gail's mouth dropped open. 'Ten quid, that's a fortune! Where did it come from?'

Ellen shook her head. 'Goodness only knows what else she'd been up to. I'll put it in the office for now.'

Pulling open another drawer, Gail drew in a breath. 'There's more here.'

In total there was thirty pounds, an unbelievable amount to be carelessly strewn in the dresser. Ellen blew out her cheeks as she stared at the cash. 'I'll pay for the funeral out of it and the rest can go in the safe. Oh, that reminds me, I must put a notice in the newspaper.'

'Why bother? Kathy never had a visitor all the time she was here. No letters either.'

'That's true, but some people just like to attend funerals, it's like a day out for them.'

'That's macabre,' Gail muttered as they left the room looking like it had never been used.

Ellen locked away the money and Gail threw out Kathy's tattered clothes. Later that day, Gail told Jess and Carter about the fortune Kathy had stashed away in the old dresser. They were shocked and could shed no light on how the cleaner had come by so much money but all of them assumed the worst.

* * *

On the day of the funeral, Ellen closed the pub and, dressed in black, the residents of the pub followed the horse-drawn hearse to St Bartholomew's Church. As Ellen predicted there were folk in attendance who had not even known Kathy Frith.

At the close of the short service, the coffin was lowered into the grave and as the gravediggers began to fill in the hole, a young woman approached.

'Are you Ellen Marsh?' she asked the landlady.

'I am.'

'I'm Lucy Frith, Kathy's sister.'

'I… I'm sorry, I was led to believe Kathy was an orphan.'

Gail and Jess exchanged a look of shock at the revelation.

'As you can see, she was not.'

'Excuse me,' Jess interrupted, 'but how do we know you are who you say you are?'

'Ah, Jess Lacey, I presume,' Lucy said, looking down her nose.

'Yes, that's right.' Jess bristled at the tone used by the stranger.

'Gail Henley,' the woman went on, 'and you must be Carter Adams.'

'How is it you know us when we've never heard of you?' Carter asked.

'Kathy wrote to me often telling me all about each of you,' Lucy said pointedly.

Jess gave an involuntary shiver. If what this woman said was true, what else had Kathy divulged in her letters?

'Miss Frith, I suggest you accompany us back to the pub where we can discuss this in more privacy,' Ellen said.

With a nod, Lucy Frith fell into step alongside Ellen.

38

Gail had prepared a small buffet for the wake, and once everyone was in the kitchen she made tea.

'Now, Miss Frith, I would be obliged if you could provide some proof of identity,' Ellen said sternly.

Clearly Lucy had expected this and from her bag she pulled out two birth certificates, hers and Kathy's.

After looking them over, Ellen then passed the papers to the others for inspection.

'I don't know what to say,' Ellen said, returning the certificates to Lucy.

'First of all, I expect the money sent to Kathy by our father to be repaid in full.'

'I have Kathy's savings in the safe. I'll get them for you now.' Ellen rushed from the kitchen and returned a moment later. 'Thirty pounds less the cost of the funeral; the paperwork is there too.'

Lucy cast her eyes over the invoice from Webb's, marked as paid in full. That, along with the money, she pushed into her bag without a word of thanks. 'Now I'd like to know how my sister died.'

Ellen related the events of the fateful night, feeling uncomfortable under Lucy's stare.

'I believe you and Kathy were to be married, Mr Adams.'

'No. I'm afraid Kathy thought so but it's not true. I never gave her any encouragement as Jess and I are...'

'I see. So you're saying my sister was a liar?' Lucy snapped.

'No, Miss Frith, she was mistaken. Kathy was poorly in her mind, I'm sorry to say,' Carter corrected the severe woman.

'And was she seen by a doctor?'

'No. What is it you want from us, Miss Frith?' Carter asked, refusing to be cowed by this young woman.

'I want the truth, Mr Adams.'

'You have it, every word.'

With a curt nod, Lucy Frith then turned to Jess. 'Now to you, Mrs Jess Lacey. You are a widow, are you not?'

'Yes, not that it's any of your business,' Jess said, feeling affronted. She wondered what else this woman knew about them all.

'I heard tell your husband was murdered,' Lucy probed.

'Look here, Miss Frith, you have Kathy's money so I'd be obliged if you would leave now.' Ellen got to her feet and opened the back door.

Lucy Frith marched from the room without a word or a backwards glance.

Closing the door, Ellen retook her seat at the table with a huge sigh.

'I don't trust that one,' Gail said.

'Nor me,' Ellen agreed, 'but the birth certificates looked genuine as you saw for yourself.'

'I don't mean that. I'm worried she knows more than she was letting on,' Gail clarified.

'That thought crossed my mind too,' Jess put in. 'She knew about Bill's death, but is she aware of who caused it?'

Ellen groaned. 'We should have found out where she lived.'

'It wouldn't have done any good,' Carter said.

'Why not?' asked Jess.

'Because I have a feeling we might be seeing Lucy Frith again,' he replied.

It was Gail's turn to groan, her head now in her hands.

However, when the next weeks passed without incident, everyone at the pub began to relax at hearing nothing more from Lucy Frith.

* * *

Lady Autumn painted the trees with gold and brown and slowly then relinquished their hold on the leaves. Fluttering quietly to the ground, they formed colourful carpets at the base of the trees which were preparing for their long winter sleep.

Sweeps were out in force, clearing chimneys in readiness for the chilly days to come. Women all over the town were pickling and bottling fruits and vegetables to see them through until spring came round again.

Although the sun still shone, its rays weakened with each passing day. Summer attire was packed away in favour of warmer clothes, boots replaced, shoes and jackets and gloves were donned.

Without even realising, the people of Birmingham were getting ready for the onslaught of raging winds, falling temperatures and snow-laden streets.

Due to their busy schedule behind the bar, Jess and Carter's relationship was reduced to loving glances and the occasional touch of each other's hand.

The little coterie at the pub had discussed Lucy Frith and reached a consensus that Peg and Jim Butler did not need to know about the woman. There had been no further communication from Miss Frith, and everyone prayed it would stay that way.

* * *

Over in Wednesbury, Peg was in her element, selling luxurious garments to those with the money to buy them. The burden of Jim's guilt had been lifted with the death of the cleaner, and Peg had pushed it from her mind. Her man was safe and she revelled in the freedom from worry.

Jim and his friends had also stopped fretting that they could be arrested at any moment. Jim had taken his revenge on his neighbour who had hurt Peg so badly, and the blackmailing Kathy Frith had joined Bill Lacey in the afterlife. Therefore for Jim, the matter was now closed. He could get on with living life with his beautiful wife, without a care in the world.

39

On a clement October morning, a well-dressed older man strode into the bar.

'What can I get you?' Carter asked.

Removing his top hat, the man said, 'I'm looking for Ellen Marsh.'

'Who shall I say is asking for her?'

'My name is Henry Frith.'

Doing his best to hide his shock, Carter gave a nod and went to find Ellen.

Jess felt her insides turn over as she glanced at the man who could only be Kathy's father.

Sitting at their usual table, Bella and Enid watched in silence.

'Please come through, sir,' Carter said and led the visitor to the kitchen where he was greeted by Ellen. 'Will you take tea?' she asked as she motioned for him to sit.

'Thank you, that would be most enjoyable.'

Gail set about providing refreshments as she listened intently.

'How can I help you, Mr Frith?' Ellen asked.

'I saw the announcement in the newspaper of Kathy's passing. I was away on business in France and couldn't get back in time for the funeral. Please don't think me impertinent but I understand my daughter, Kathy, worked for you.'

'She did and I am sorry for your loss,' Ellen said. 'How did you know she was here?'

'Thank you. I spent a lot of time asking around until someone informed me of her whereabouts. Kathy was not the easiest of people to get on with,' he said sadly. Gail poured tea for them all and Mr Frith thanked the cook as she cut cake before sitting at the table. 'Kathy had – how can I put this – she had bad connections in her brain. At least that's how the doctors described it to me when she was young. She was always running away from home.' He paused to sip his tea then, pointing to the cake, asked, 'May I?'

'Please do, and while you eat, I can explain about Kathy being here with us,' Ellen said. Henry nodded. 'Kathy came to us some while ago. The cabbies around here know that I run this pub but it's also a refuge for people in dire straits. Your daughter was rescued from living hand-to-mouth and sleeping in doorways by my brother who is a cabbie. He brought her to me and I gave her food, lodging and a paid job of cleaner.'

Henry accepted more tea from Gail as he listened.

'Unfortunately Kathy became fixated on Carter, our barman. She was happy to sit in the bar in the evenings and watch him work. Until, that is, Jess Lacey joined us.'

'Jess?' Frith looked at Gail.

'No, I'm Gail the cook. Jess is the barmaid.'

'Ah, the girl out front,' he said.

'Jess was fleeing a violent husband and my brother brought

her here too,' Ellen went on. 'When Jess's husband was found dead, she and Carter began a relationship. Kathy became very jealous and her drinking increased.'

'I feared that might be the case. er mother went the same way, I'm afraid,' Henry explained.

'Kathy was blackmailing Jess, saying she would tell the police Jess had murdered her husband unless Jess gave her money. A baseless accusation, of course, but Jess didn't feel able to risk the police taking her side.'

Henry sighed and shook his head. 'I will repay whatever she took from Mrs Lacey.'

Ellen waved away the offer. 'Kathy then gave Carter an ultimatum – marry her or be implicated in the murder too.'

'Oh, dear Lord!' Henry closed his eyes tight for a second before looking once more at Ellen.

'She told everyone in the bar that she and Carter were betrothed and continued to drink gin like someone dying of thirst.'

'That was her mother's tipple,' Henry whispered.

'Kathy was so drunk the night she died that Gail had to help her to bed.'

Gail took over the telling of the sorry tale. 'With difficulty I got her up the stairs and I left her leaning on the banister while I opened her bedroom door. The next thing I know there's a scream and as I turned, I saw her tumble down the stairs.' Gail forced tears to her eyes and with a croak she went on. 'There was nothing I could do! I couldn't get to her in time.'

'Please don't upset yourself, I'm sure you did all you could,' Henry said, patting Gail's arm.

Oh, I certainly did, Gail thought as she blinked away the crocodile tears.

'Miss Marsh, I don't know if you are aware but each week I deposited some money for Kathy in the bank which according to the manager she withdrew...'

'I know, Mr Frith, and it was handed over to Lucy after the funeral.'

'Lucy?' he asked.

'Yes, Kathy's sister,' Ellen said, suddenly feeling very uncomfortable.

'Kathy didn't have a sister, Miss Marsh, she was an only child.'

Ellen and Gail exchanged an astonished look. 'I don't understand, this Lucy had both birth certificates as proof,' Ellen said.

'Easily obtained, I'm afraid. How much did you give her?'

'Thirty pounds less the cost of the funeral. Mr Frith, I'm so sorry, she was so convincing!'

'No matter. It seems a young woman has been duping the bereaved all over the place according to the newspapers. Maybe this woman purporting to be Kathy's sister is the same person. I believe the constabulary are on to her but they are always a step behind.'

'Good grief!' Gail exclaimed. 'Wait a minute, this woman said things that no one but a sister would know.'

'Like what?'

'That you sent her money. She knew us all by name and our business, saying Kathy had written to her,' Ellen said.

Suddenly the colour drained from Henry Frith's face.

'Sir, are you unwell?' Gail asked.

'I have to get home at once!' Henry rushed out of the room with muttered thanks.

'What the hell was all that about?' Gail asked.

'I have absolutely no idea,' Ellen returned. 'Wait 'til Jess and Carter hear about it.'

The barman and barmaid weren't the only two to be intrigued by the toff dashing out of the pub. Bella and Enid glanced at each other before putting their heads together to discuss who the gent might be, and what he was after in a place like The Queen's Head.

40

Jess and Carter stared in wide-eyed disbelief as Ellen explained the whole debacle once the pub was shut for the night.

'Well, whoever this Lucy was she came over as very well versed. She certainly had me convinced,' Carter said.

'Confident too. She fooled us all,' Jess added. 'Poor Mr Frith, he lost all that money.'

'He dashed from here like a cat with its tail on fire,' Gail put in.

'Why?' asked Jess.

'We don't know,' Ellen answered, 'but there's nothing we can do about it now so I suggest we carry on as normal.'

A week later, as breakfast was being served, Ellen slapped the newspaper she had been reading on the kitchen table. 'Listen to this!' Finding the article, she read aloud.

'On the eighteenth day of October in the year of our Lord 1889, a young woman by the name of Elsie Crowther was arrested at the place of employment where she was maid to the honourable Mr Henry Frith. Crowther, accused of obtaining money by fraudulent means from bereaved families, was taken before the magistrate. The case was moved to the Assizes where Crowther admitted to the crimes of fraud and theft. She showed no remorse for the distress she had caused grieving families. She was sentenced to ten years' hard labour.' Ellen looked up at the shocked faces around the table. 'At least now we know why Henry Frith ran from here in such a hurry,' she said.

'The maid?' Jess questioned.

'That's what the paper says.'

'What are the odds of it being Frith's maid doing all that stealing?' Gail asked.

'I can't help but worry. Did Kathy treat her like a sister and write to her about all of us, do you think? She certainly seemed to know a lot about us and had no hesitation in stealing money.' Jess's words prompted all eyes to turn to her. 'If she and Kathy were close, did Kathy mention Jim?'

Once more, the heavy feeling of foreboding settled on the four friends. Of course Kathy may never have put anything in writing to Elsie; it wouldn't have taken much for the maid to find out the names of those living and working at the pub. After all, Henry Frith had managed it so Crowther could have done the same. The odd question here and there would have provided her with the information she needed. Then it was just a matter of having the gall to carry out her objective. Unfortunately, her nefarious work had been too close to home and had seen her caught by the police. By the time Crowther was released from prison, she would be a middle-aged woman with a criminal record.

Jess pondered, how then would Crowther find a job? In short, it would be impossible. She would likely return to stealing or possibly find herself working the streets in order to survive.

It was Carter who broke the silence. 'I expect we'll know soon enough if the coppers come calling again.'

'Should we forewarn Jim and Peg?' Jess asked.

'No, there's no point in them worrying too,' Ellen replied. 'We just have to wait and see what, if anything, happens.'

'I can't believe all this has come about because I landed on your doorstep.' Tears filled Jess's eyes as she spoke.

'Don't blame yourself, Jess. It was your husband who set things in motion.' Carter placed his arm around her shoulder.

'I know that really, but I'm just so tired of it all. Just when I think we can relax, Bill raises his frightening head again,' she replied on a sob.

'Look, why don't you two go out tonight? I can manage the bar...' Ellen began.

'And I can help,' Gail put in.

'That would be nice, thank you.' Jess dried her tears and smiled as Carter kissed her cheek tenderly.

Gail packed them a small picnic basket and the couple set off for the music hall.

Entering through the double doors, Carter purchased two tickets before leading Jess into the theatre proper. Finding their seats, they settled to listen to the small orchestra tuning up their instruments. Every now and then they stood to allow others to pass to get to their own seats. The gas lights on the walls dimmed and the music began to thunderous applause.

A man walked on stage and a hush fell over the audience. 'Ladies and gentlemen, please give a warm welcome to George Fellows!' More applause as Mr Fellows walked to centre stage.

'I said to my wife, this vinegar has lumps in it. She replied, "That's because they're pickled onions!"'

Polite laughter was heard and Fellows tried again. 'I told her

I'm a millionaire, haven't I got enough for both of us? Her answer was, "Yes, if you are moderate in your tastes."'

His joke was met with groans and unfortunately the longer he went on, the worse it became until someone threw a scrap of food, hitting him on the forehead. Fellows covered his head with his arms as he scampered back to the wings.

Next came the Rialto Brothers, acrobats. One climbed onto the shoulders of the other, the one supporting beginning to stagger under the weight of his companion. The audience drew in a breath, expecting a fall, but the brothers maintained their balance. With a bend of his knees, the supporter tossed the other into the air where he spun before landing on the boards with a thud. Everyone clapped as they continued to throw each other around, eliciting oohs and ahhs from the public.

This was followed by a Miss Phoebe Martinez, who sang beautifully before inviting the audience to join in with some of the most popular songs.

A Lion Comique in the style of George Laybourne, who had died some years previously, began to sing 'Champagne Charlie', much to the delight of the punters.

There was a plate spinner, a stilt walker and a trick cyclist, all of whom left the stage to loud clapping and whistling.

The lights came up again, denoting an interval, and the theatre filled with conversations and laughter. Carter and Jess discussed the acts they'd seen. Jess opened the basket and pulled out ham and mustard sandwiches, lemonade and two small glasses. There was pork pie and also some fruit for afters. Most attending the music hall would take a picnic to enjoy during the break, almost always keeping back some food to be thrown at the acts they thought to be not so good. It was all part of the theatre-going experience.

Again the lights lowered and another singer was introduced.

Later came a juggler who was pelted with orange peel and scraps of food for dropping his juggling pins more than once. A ventriloquist pleased the audience and he was followed by a mime act who was booed off stage.

Eventually the raising of the lights informed the public it was time to go home and Jess and Carter stood to leave. They wove their way through the crowds and sauntered home, chatting happily.

The couple had enjoyed their evening at the music hall, feeling finally they were able to relax a little.

It was on their return home that they learned of a murder having taken place.

* * *

Bella and Enid were sitting in the kitchen after The Queen's Head had closed for the night.

'One of the girls was found with her throat cut!' Bella gasped.

'Good grief! How terrible!' Ellen exclaimed.

'When was this?' Jess asked.

'They found her this morning. We've been interviewed by the coppers, one by one, all day,' Enid explained.

'We thought, at first, that it might have been Jack the Ripper come up from London...' Bella said.

'But they don't believe it was,' Enid took over. 'There were no mutilations apparently.'

Jess shivered involuntarily as she listened. 'Do the police have any idea who the perpetrator might be?'

'No. They ain't got a clue.'

'I thought you ladies worked in pairs after Enid got battered,' Gail said.

'We do, but Trixie decided to go it alone. Her mate heard the man offer her a quid before they went off together.'

'A pound! That's a lot of money,' Carter added.

'Exactly. Who's likely to turn that down?' Bella said. 'The other thing is, the fella spoke with an accent that Enid had heard before.'

Everyone looked at Enid, who nodded. 'Seems it could be the same bloke who beat me up.'

'You really were lucky that night then, Enid,' Jess said.

'Don't I bloody know it!'

'Anyway,' Bella took up, 'the coppers have warned us to stay off the streets until this man is caught.'

'That sounds like a very sensible idea,' Ellen agreed.

'It is, but what will you do about money?' Jess asked.

'We've both got some savings but they won't last long. Eventually we'll be forced out onto the streets again,' Bella stated.

'I have an opening for a cleaner,' Ellen suggested, 'but that would only help one of you.'

'I'll tek it with thanks,' Enid said hastily.

'Ellen, we could do with extra help behind the bar. If you could see your way clear to hiring Bella, I'd be happy to take a cut in wages,' Jess said.

'You're right about us being very busy and needing another pair of hands, I don't know why I didn't think of it myself.' Ellen slapped her forehead. 'How do you fancy it, Bella?'

'I thank you but not if it means Jess loses money.'

'She won't. There's no need, I can more than cover the earnings.'

'Then you have yourself a deal.'

The happy band celebrated with cups of tea and lemon drizzle cake, relieved to know that their friends wouldn't have to face the dangerous streets that night or for the foreseeable future.

41

Bella and Enid had been in their new jobs but a few days when a police sergeant and two constables came calling. Once they'd been shown into the kitchen, the sergeant began. 'I'm here to speak with Mrs Jess Lacey.'

'That's me.' Jess felt her nerves jangle.

'I'm Sergeant Phillips. It appears, Mrs Lacey, that you may have been complicit in the murder of your husband.'

'What?' Jess sat down heavily on a kitchen chair, feeling shocked to her core.

Gail and Ellen exchanged a glance and Carter drew in a noisy breath.

'I didn't kill my husband, sergeant! What a terrible thing to imply.'

'We don't believe you killed him,' the man replied firmly.

Gail lifted the teapot and the sergeant nodded, then he and his constables sat at the table.

'Then what do you mean...?' Jess asked on a breath.

'Let me explain first of all that although a case might be closed, any new evidence or leads must be followed up.'

'Do you have new evidence, sergeant?' Carter asked.

'We have in our possession a number of letters in which you, Mrs Lacey, are accused of being in league with another person for the sole purpose of disposing of your spouse.'

'Who is this other person?' Jess asked, trying to keep her composure.

'We were not given a name...'

Jess was relieved that Jim had not been mentioned in the correspondence at least.

'Where did the letters come from?' Ellen asked.

'Mr Henry Frith.'

'Kathy's father,' Jess said quietly.

'Yes, I believe Kathy Frith was a cleaner here,' the sergeant confirmed.

'She was,' Ellen said. 'I'm afraid we lost her a little while ago.'

'Indeed, Mr Frith informed us of her demise. As it turned out, it seems Kathy and Mr Frith's maid, Elsie Crowther, were very close. Whenever Kathy ran away from home, she would always write to the maid telling her where she was and about the people she met.'

'We read about the maid in the newspaper, Elsie Crowther being arrested, I mean,' Carter said.

'Apparently the maid and her mistress were in cahoots. They worked together to blackmail folk out of their hard-earned money, mostly they targeted bereaved families.'

'Good grief! How awful!' Jess exclaimed.

'We have piles of letters as proof of their nefarious deeds.'

'So, if you don't believe I killed Bill...' Jess began.

'Like I said, I have to follow up on any new leads, as with all the other correspondence. It's gonna take forever,' he sighed, 'but it's all part of the job.'

'Cake, sergeant?' Gail asked.

'I won't say no, thank you.'

With Bella on the bar and Enid cleaning the bedrooms, everyone else was sitting or standing with the police in the kitchen. For all the world it looked like a tea party.

When they had finished their refreshments, the sergeant got to his feet. 'Thank you for the tea. We'll be on our way now.'

'Sergeant, you don't think Jess was involved in all this, do you?' Carter asked.

'No, sir, we don't,' he replied. 'You can rest easy.'

Carter saw them out and on his return he blew out his cheeks. 'That was close.'

'I thought they were here to arrest me,' Jess mumbled.

'As did we all for a minute,' Ellen confessed.

'At least Jim is in the clear,' Gail added.

'Yes, that's a weight off my mind,' Jess agreed.

'Well, I'm guessing that's the last we'll hear of it all,' Ellen said.

'I hope so because my nerves are shredded,' Jess replied.

'Now we can get on with our lives once and for all,' Carter said.

'I'll drink to that,' Jess said, raising her teacup.

A frown creased Carter's forehead and he said, 'Hang on. If Kathy wrote to Elsie Crowther, surely she would have received replies.'

'We didn't find anything when we cleared Kathy's room,' Ellen stated, 'and she didn't have any letters delivered here.'

'Maybe she collected them from the Post Office,' Gail suggested.

'If that's the case, where are they now?' Jess asked.

'Maybe we should check Kathy's room again,' Carter said.

'We were very thorough when we cleared the room out. I don't think we would have missed letters,' Ellen protested.

'I know, but think about it. Kathy and Elsie Crowther had been blackmailing people for some time according to the sergeant. It stands to reason they were very proficient at it, so I'm thinking Kathy would have found a safe place to hide anything that could have incriminated her.'

'Where though?' Jess asked.

'There's only one way to find out. Ellen, come with me, we're going hunting.' Carter got to his feet and he and Ellen left the kitchen to search Kathy's room yet again.

'I was so afraid when the police came,' Jess confessed to the cook.

'Me too,' Gail concurred.

Jess glanced at her friend as she wondered why Gail was worried. A thought flitted through her mind – had Gail fretted the police had come for her because she'd pushed Kathy to her death? Dismissing the idea as impossible, Jess was sure Gail was only worried on her behalf.

Upstairs, Ellen and Carter looked everywhere for anything relating to Kathy and Elsie's blackmail plots. Just as they were about to give up, Carter's eye was drawn to the carpet near the door. The edge was frayed and as he approached he saw that it was no longer tacked to the floorboards.

Ellen watched as he pulled back the carpet. 'Hello, what do we have here?' he said. Lifting a loose board, he smiled. Reaching into the cavity, he withdrew a stack of envelopes and passed them to Ellen.

'Blimey!' Ellen gasped.

'Do you recognise this?' Carter asked, holding up a necklace of pearls.

'Yes, it's mine! I wondered what had happened to it. I had just decided I must have mislaid it.'

Carter pulled out earrings, bracelets, rings and a wad of money.

'The thieving mare!' Ellen said sharply.

'If it's not yours then the jewellery should go to the police, maybe the sergeant can find the owners.'

'No, the rest of those belongings are not mine, only the pearls belong to me. I think we should go and read these letters before we decide what to do with them.'

Carter nodded, replaced the floorboard and carpet, then followed Ellen back down to the kitchen.

42

One by one, the letters were read aloud by Ellen and they were all surprised by the amount of information contained in each missive. Elsie Crowther had agreed that Carter, she was sure, would propose to Kathy before too long. Ellen, she said, was a soft touch, taking in anyone who she thought wanted help. A fair employer maybe, but Ellen was very rich and a plan was needed to relieve her of all of her money. Kathy had clearly described Gail as a bit of a nonentity, although she had at least stated that she was a good cook.

At that, Gail clenched her teeth to prevent her saying something she would regret. In her mind, Gail thought, *you dismissed me as nothing, didn't you, Kathy? That was your first big mistake, lady!*

Kathy had evidently gone on to speak of Jess, the girl she felt was trying to steal Carter away from her. She must have laid out what she knew of Bill Lacey's murder, and that Jess had been the instigator. From Elsie Crowther's replies, the little coterie could guess pretty accurately what Kathy had written.

'Why did Kathy not name Jim?' Jess asked.

'Maybe she was holding that snippet in abeyance for when she came for me and my money,' Ellen said.

'It looks to me like Kathy was the puppet and Elsie Crowther was pulling the strings,' Carter said as he piled up the correspondence.

'So, what happens now?' Gail asked.

'The letters and the jewellery should be taken to the sergeant at the police station,' Jess answered. 'I'll do it first thing tomorrow.'

'I'll come with you,' Carter said as he laid a protective hand on her arm.

'Right, that's the bedrooms done,' Enid said as she bustled into the kitchen. 'Ellen, them carpets upstairs are dangerous, I nearly broke my bloody neck!'

'Which carpets?' Ellen questioned.

'All of them.'

Carter and Ellen exchanged a look then together they stood and left the kitchen.

Enid gave Jess a puzzled glance, at which Jess shrugged her shoulders.

Just then, Bella's booming voice sailed into the kitchen. 'Some help needed in the bar, please!'

'I'll go,' Enid said, to Jess's surprise.

'What do you make of all this?' Gail asked, pointing to the jewellery and letters.

'I can hardly believe it. Kathy and Crowther must have been in league for years, duping people out of their money and valuables.'

'The coppers have a job on their hands getting it all back to the owners,' Gail responded.

'They'll need a dedicated team, I would think. Like the

sergeant said, it could take an age to complete such a task.' Jess shook her head at the thought.

Upstairs, Ellen and Carter started their search in his room. They quickly found the loose carpet and prised up the floorboard.

'Oh, Lord!' Ellen said as he pulled out more jewellery and small trinkets. 'We're going to need a box, I think.'

Whilst Carter emptied the cavity, Ellen went to her room then returned with a large hat box.

'Gail's room next,' Carter said as he replaced the board and carpet. 'When we've done, I'll tack the carpets down again.'

By the time they came to Jess's room, the last to be searched, the hat box was almost full. Beneath Jess's floor, Carter found rolls of money amounting to around fifty pounds.

'Where did Kathy get all this from?' Ellen queried.

'Her father over years and years would be my guess,' Carter said, tamping down the floor covering. 'At least, I hope so.'

Returning downstairs to the kitchen, Ellen placed the box on the table.

'Good grief!' Jess gasped as she eyed the contents.

'I was thinking more like bloody hell!' Gail said with a shocked laugh.

'We're assuming the money most likely came from Kathy's father,' Ellen said.

'Then it should be returned to him,' Jess answered.

'We don't know where he lives,' Carter said.

'The sergeant would be able to tell us, I'm sure,' Ellen supplied as she placed the jewels and letters into the box before putting the lid on firmly. 'For now, I suggest we get back to work, then in the morning, this goes to the constabulary.' Ellen tapped the box as the others nodded their agreement.

* * *

After breakfast the following day, Carter and Jess boarded a cab to the police station, the hat box carried by Carter and placed firmly on his lap.

Even with her coat on, Jess gave a shiver. It wasn't the chill that had started to settle in to the autumn days, however, but the thought of having to deal with the constabulary again. All the while in the back of her mind was the worry that they would discover her friend, Jim, had murdered her husband.

On their arrival at the station, they asked to speak with the sergeant.

'May I ask what it's about?' the constable on the duty desk asked.

'If you just tell him we're here regarding Elsie Crowther,' Carter replied.

'If you'll wait a moment...' The young man rushed away to return a moment later with Sergeant Phillips.

'Please come this way,' the officer said.

The sergeant showed them into a small room, then indicated the chairs, and before sitting Carter placed the box on the table.

'Now, I believe your visit has to do with the Crowther case?'

'Yes,' Carter said. 'After you left The Queen's Head, it occurred to us we may be wise to search Kathy's room...' He related the events of searching and discovering the letters, jewels and money. Lifting the lid of the box, Carter pushed it across the table towards the policeman.

Sergeant Phillips's eyes peeped into the box then tipped up to look at the couple sitting opposite him. With a huge sigh, he blew out his cheeks. Clearly he didn't relish the task that lay before him. His shoulders slumped and he hung his head, chin to chest. With a breath, he looked up once more. 'I thank you for… this,' he said, pointing to the box, 'we will do our best to get it all back to the owners, though God only knows how.'

'We think the money must belong to Mr Frith,' Jess said. 'He told us he sent Kathy some each week.'

With a nod, the sergeant replied, 'I'll see that he gets it. Thank you both, you can leave everything to us now.'

Jess and Carter were shown out and, as Carter looked around for a cab, Jess said, 'I feel a little deflated now.'

'I know what you mean. We've lived on our nerves for such a long time and now quite suddenly it's all over,' Carter replied as he waved to a cabbie.

'At least we have lots to tell Peg and Jim when next we see them.'

'Indeed,' was all Carter said as he helped Jess into the carriage.

43

Before they'd had time to pull away, Jess exclaimed, 'I've had an idea!' and climbed out onto the pavement once more.

'We'll be just a moment,' Carter called to the cabbie.

'Very good, sir.'

Carter followed Jess back into the station where the sergeant was still speaking with the duty constable.

'Sergeant, may I have a word, please?'

With a nod, Sergeant Phillips led them back to the little room where the hat box still sat on the table, a constable on guard by the door.

Jess explained what she had in mind to the astonishment of both Carter and the policeman.

'That would be most irregular,' the sergeant said at last. 'It's evidence, you see.' He tilted his head to the box.

'Elsie Crowther has been tried and convicted, sergeant, therefore surely your staff would be returning the *evidence* to the people it belongs to.'

'Well, yes, but...'

'How many of your constables would be taken from their regular duties to do that?' Jess asked.

'I don't know offhand, but I concur it would be a fair number,' the sergeant replied, rubbing his whiskers.

'With my idea, you wouldn't have to use any of them,' Jess stated.

'I would need to speak with my superior about it...'

'We can wait,' Jess said firmly.

Mumbling under his breath, the sergeant left them.

'Jess, I'm not sure this is such a good idea,' Carter whispered.

'Why not?'

'What about our jobs at the pub? Ellen could sack us!'

'You know she won't.'

A moment later, the sergeant returned with another man dressed in plain clothes. 'This is Detective Inspector Drake,' he said. 'Inspector, meet Jess Lacey and Carter Adams.'

'The sergeant has told me about your idea regarding returning the stolen items to their respective owners,' the Detective Inspector said.

'If Carter and I took on the task then your officers would be free to go about their business,' Jess said quickly.

'Miss Lacey...'

'Mrs,' Jess corrected.

'Mrs Lacey, you can see the problem here, I'm sure. We don't know you from Adam. From Adams, get it?' He said, tittering at his own joke.

'That's true, but if we wanted to steal all that stuff then why would we bring it here in the first place?'

'She has a point, sir,' Sergeant Phillips said.

'I can't see how we could allow it, sergeant.'

'Perhaps you could give us special dispensation in the form of a letter or card for the duration of the task.'

The Detective Inspector paced the room as he considered the proposal.

Jess pressed on as her excitement began to build. 'We could have people sign a ledger as proof that they had received their items.'

'I'm tempted to...' the Inspector began.

'You won't regret it if you agree, sir, I promise,' Jess pushed.

'Give us a moment.' He and his sergeant left the room and Jess drummed her fingers on the table impatiently.

The next five minutes seemed like an eternity but eventually the policemen returned. Two letters of authorisation were laid on the table.

Jess couldn't believe what she was seeing and Carter's mouth dropped open.

The sergeant provided two police ledgers, two fountain pens and a bottle of ink.

'This is an unprecedented risk I'm taking here. We are trusting you with this, Mrs Lacey. If it should come to pass that you break this trust, I will personally hunt you down and see you in jail for the rest of your life. Do you understand?'

'Yes, Detective Inspector Drake, completely. I propose that once a week we bring the ledgers to the station to be signed off by Sergeant Phillips. That way you will be assured of our intent to complete the job assigned to us.'

Carter was shocked to his core and found himself quite unable to speak. He nodded along to the conversation like an automaton.

'Very well. The sergeant will provide you with the letters found at Crowther's address. You will need them in order to try and match the stolen goods to the victims.'

'Thank you, Detective Inspector,' Jess said.

'Remember what I said, Mrs Lacey, because I'm going out on a limb here with this idea of yours.'

'We won't let you down, sir.'

Drake nodded and walked out followed by the sergeant.

Jess read the document giving them authorisation as temporary police assistants.

When the sergeant returned, he was carrying a large box which he set on the table. 'Everything you need is in there. Be advised, Mrs Lacey, our Detective Inspector Drake can be an absolute stinker if crossed.'

'Duly noted, sergeant. If you need us, we'll be at The Queen's Head. Thank you for your trust in this matter.'

'Good luck, judging by that lot you're going to need it.'

Carrying the boxes, ledgers, pens, ink, and letters, Carter and Jess left the station and climbed into the waiting cab.

'The Queen's Head, please,' Carter called out, finally finding his tongue.

As the cab pulled away, he looked at the boxes then at Jess's smiling face. He shook his head then burst out laughing, still unable to believe what Jess had got him into.

44

In his office, Detective Inspector Drake said, 'Sergeant Phillips, do you think I've done the right thing?'

'Buggered if I know, beggin' your pardon, sir, but it does spare my lads from a back-breaking stint in the station. We've a murderer on the loose still and I know they would rather be out there looking for him. Anyway, you'll know by next week.'

'How so?'

'The intrepid duo should be reporting in, sir.'

The Inspector nodded with his mouth screwed up tightly. Then muttered, 'Adams and Lacey.'

'Sounds like one of those penny dreadful books off the market. I'll keep you up to date, sir,' Sergeant Phillips said before leaving the office.

Drake spent the next half an hour tapping a pencil on his desk, silently praying Lacey and Adams had not taken him for a fool.

* * *

Over at The Queen's Head, Jess was explaining the two boxes of items, letters and police reports. 'It means we can't work the bar for a while though, Ellen,' she said.

'Bella and Enid have the bar covered so don't worry about that, but you have your work cut out returning all these items and no mistake,' Ellen replied.

'I can't believe the police are allowing you to do this,' Gail said.

'I know, I didn't think they were going to at one point,' Jess answered. Then to Carter she went on, 'We'll need to sort through everything first and try and match items to areas to save legwork.'

'I have a map we can use,' Carter said helpfully.

'Let's take the boxes up to my room...' Jess began as she lifted the hat box.

'Why not use the room Carol had before she left?' Ellen suggested.

'Good idea,' Jess replied, 'we'll have more space in there.'

Upstairs, Jess was getting organised. 'We need to be methodical about this, Carter. Letters in one pile in order of date, and reports in another. If stolen items are listed anywhere we can match them straight away. That will give us a starting point.'

'We'd best get on with it then,' Carter said, followed by a sigh as he opened the box given to them by Sergeant Phillips.

The two worked for a while and eventually the paperwork was stacked in neat piles. Gail brought up a tea tray, saying dinner wouldn't be long. Now they were ready to get to the bottom of things. Carter and Jess each read a letter as they sipped their tea then checked it against the police reports. Jess quickly realised there were far more letters than reports and that their job was going to be a lot harder than she had first anticipated.

'I'm guessing a lot of people just paid the blackmail money and didn't involve the police,' Jess said.

'According to this paperwork, the coppers were only told of the theft of jewellery and trinkets, and even then not in all cases,' Carter replied.

Taking a break for a meal, Jess told their friends all about their plan of action and how they were getting on so far. After dinner, the pair retired to the bedroom once more, where they sat to read through the letters from Kathy and, where they could, pin Crowther's reply to each one. Then they matched any clues from the letters to areas on the map. Slowly the whole sorry saga took on a shape and began to make sense. Some items were paired using the description the victim had given to the police. These more simple examples would be where they would start in their quest.

To keep track of their findings, firstly Jess ruled three columns on the right-hand side of the pages of the ledgers. One for the owner's signature, the second for her or Carter's initials, and the third for Sergeant Phillips to sign. Then she wrote a brief outline of each item; gold ring – emerald stone, silver chain and locket, silver snuff box.

Meanwhile, Carter was drawing out a grid on the map and checking any addresses found in the documentation. Then he suddenly sat up. 'Have you noticed how quiet it is?'

Jess looked up too. 'Bella must have closed up for the night. We've been working for hours. Let's leave this and go down for tea with the others.'

Carter yawned, only then realising how tired he was.

Over refreshments, Jess and Carter told all the pub's residents about their day's work.

'So you'm coppers now then?' Enid asked.

Jess laughed. 'No, we're just helping the police to try and reunite victims with their stolen goods.'

'Then you'm bobbies in my eyes. Hey, Bella, it's a good job we ain't on the streets no more else they could arrest us!'

'No, Enid, we couldn't. We don't have the power to arrest anyone,' Carter emphasised.

'Working the bar is preferable to standing street corners, I have to say,' Bella put in, 'and on that note I think it's time we went home. I'm exhausted from serving behind the bar all day.'

'Do you want me to walk with you?' Carter asked.

'No, lovey, we'll be fine but thanks for the offer.' Bella nudged her friend and the two women donned their coats and left via the back door.

'Oh, I'm exhausted too, so I'm for bed.' Ellen yawned.

'Me too,' Gail agreed.

Alone in the kitchen at last, Jess and Carter were finally able to share a hug and a kiss.

'It seems forever since I held you,' he whispered.

'I know. It's been a whirlwind here and we've been so busy what with one thing and another.'

'You do know that I love you, Jess Lacey.'

With a smile, she said, 'And I love you too, Carter Adams.'

Quite suddenly, Carter dropped to one knee, taking Jess completely by surprise. 'Marry me, Jess,' he said, looking up at her. 'Please say you will.'

Looking down into his puppy-dog eyes, she smiled. She had prayed for this day for such a long time and now it was here.

'Yes, Carter, I will,' she said breathlessly.

Jumping up, he kissed her passionately before lifting her off her feet and swinging her around.

What a day it had been and Jess could only imagine the

wonderful days and years that now lay ahead, sharing a life with the man she loved.

45

The following morning, the pub was full of excited buzz and congratulations as the happy couple told their friends about their engagement. Jess said she would write to Peg with the news and Carter promised to see the vicar about a date for the wedding. He didn't see the point in waiting, but Jess requested enough time to arrange things; they still had a job to do for the police, after all.

Deciding to start straight away, Jess and Carter set out on the first of their visits as police assistants. Armed with written authority, pens and ledger as well as an envelope containing a gent's signet ring, they hailed a cab.

'Prospect Row, please,' Carter called out.

The cabbie tipped his hat and waited until his passengers were aboard before clucking to his horse.

'I'm nervous,' Jess confessed.

'Don't be, it's a good thing we're doing.'

'I know, I just hope it all goes well.'

'It will, sweetheart, have faith.'

After the short ride, the cab halted. They asked the cabbie to wait and Carter led Jess to the door of a large house. There were two steps flanked by huge pillars before reaching the door. Smoke billowed from a chimney, testament to someone being at home. Carter banged the knocker and after a moment a maid answered.

'We're here to see Mr or Mrs Montgomery,' Jess said confidently.

'Please come in.' The maid closed the door and bade them wait. She disappeared along the short corridor and reappeared a moment later following behind a lady. Short and a little dumpy with dark hair pinned up into a neat style, the woman gave a welcoming smile, immediately putting Jess and Carter at their ease.

'I'm Mrs Montgomery, how can I help you?'

Jess gave a brief explanation that they were helping the police and Mrs Montgomery turned to the maid. 'Tea in the parlour, please, Iris.' Then to Jess, 'Please come this way.'

Once they were all seated, Jess glanced around. Expensive furniture was dotted around the room and full curtains were draped at the windows. Small tables held vases of flowers or statues which Jess guessed would have cost a lot of money. A fire burned in the grate, making the room warm and cosy.

Then the woman asked. 'Now, how can I help you, officers?'

'We are police assistants, Mrs Montgomery. We are here to ask you about the ring you reported as stolen.'

'Oh, I see. Have you found it by any chance?'

'Possibly. I wonder, could you describe it for us?'

Iris, the maid, came into the room with a tea tray and left again quietly.

As she poured their drinks, Mrs Montgomery said, 'It is my husband's signet ring. It's gold with a cabochon stone of jet. It was given to him by his father.'

Jess pulled an envelope from her bag and passed it over. Slowly, cautiously, Mrs Montgomery opened the envelope and tipped the ring onto her hand. She smiled broadly. 'Yes, this is it! Oh, I can't thank you enough!'

'It's just such a pleasure to have been able to return the ring to its rightful home.' Carter's smile was as broad as Mrs Montgomery's.

Jess asked Mrs Montgomery to sign against the right listing in the ledger and then initialled in her column.

'You have quite a list there, Miss Lacey.'

Jess smiled as she accepted more tea.

'We have only just begun our task,' Carter said as he too sipped his tea. 'In fact, Mrs Montgomery, you are our first client.'

The lady inclined her head then asked, 'May I enquire as to how you found my husband's ring?'

'All we can tell you is that the person responsible is no longer in a position to steal anything else,' Jess said.

'I understand. Be assured Gerard will be delighted when he sees this ring. We can't thank you enough.'

Jess and Carter exchanged a smile and then the woman spoke again. 'I'm surprised, Miss Lacey, that the police are employing a woman.'

'They're not, strictly speaking, Mrs Montgomery. We had a run-in with the person who stole that ring and at my insistence the police allowed us to endeavour to give back what was stolen,' Jess explained.

'My dear girl, how perfectly heroic of you, both of you, in fact.'

'Thank you for your hospitality and I'm glad we were able to assist in the return of your husband's property.'

Mrs Montgomery rang for Iris to see them out, once again giving her grateful thanks.

Jess was beaming when she and Carter boarded the cab to return home.

'Well done, *Miss* Lacey, soon-to-become Mrs Adams,' Carter said, making Jess laugh.

'It was so exciting! Mrs Montgomery was so pleased, as will her husband be,' Jess said.

When they got back they told their tale to all their friends, who praised them fulsomely on completing their first assignment. Once they'd caught up on all the goings-on in the pub, Jess was keen to get back to Carol's old bedroom, now their investigation room. 'We need to work from your grid so we don't have to keep coming back and forth to the pub, otherwise it will take a lifetime to get it all done.'

'Right, let's map out what we can and then tomorrow we can return more than one item,' Carter agreed.

By the time Gail called them down for dinner, they had four places marked for visits the following day.

After eating, Carter went to check the cellar and Jess stayed in the kitchen chatting with Gail and Ellen.

A while later, Bella came through to the kitchen. 'There's a Peg here to see you, Jess.'

Jess jumped up and rushed through the bar to greet her friend and her husband. 'It's so lovely to see you both. Come to the kitchen, the others will be glad of your visit.'

Indeed they were. Tea was served and cake cut and Carter was called up from the cellar. Lively chatter rang out as they caught up on each other's news, and Jess was delighted to hear Amelia had offered Peg a partnership in her business.

'That's wonderful!' Jess gushed.

'Well, yes, but...'

'What?' Jess asked.

'I'm not sure we can afford it, but I'm happy enough as a saleswoman.'

'Peg, I have some savings, you are welcome to them,' Jess offered.

'No, darlin', you hang on to them, you've worked hard for them,' Peg said. 'Now when's this wedding of yours? Tell us everything.'

Ellen sat back and listened to her friends discussing details about the forthcoming marriage, but her mind was working overtime. She had more money than she knew what to do with, and she wanted to help Peg secure the half share in Amelia's business. How to do that without it seeming like charity, however? Clearly Peg was very proud and wouldn't accept the money as a gift, so what could Ellen do about it?

At a lull in the conversation, Ellen spoke up. 'Peg, I can give you the money to buy half of the business.'

'That's good of you, Ellen, but I couldn't accept,' Peg answered.

'Hear me out before you dismiss the offer. I propose, in exchange for the money, you outfit us all for Jess's wedding. That would include her gown and Carter's suit. Do you think Amelia would go for it?'

'Yes, probably, especially if we could advertise that we are providing attire for a wedding,' Peg said. 'I can at least ask and see what she says.'

'Good. Let me know and I'll bank transfer the money should she agree.'

'You don't know how much it is yet,' Jim put in.

'It doesn't matter, I can cover it,' Ellen said simply.

'That's very kind of you, Ellen,' Peg said. 'I was surprised when Amelia proposed the partnership because I haven't been working there very long. It seems she needs the money. Her sister, who lives in Wales, is poorly and Amelia has been visiting regularly.'

'I would imagine that would eat into her savings and it wouldn't be cheap,' Ellen replied.

'Exactly. To be honest, I can see her selling up in the end and moving to be with her sister. Nothing has been said but if I don't take her offer then I suspect that's what she'll do.'

'Even if you agree to become a partner, she could still sell her half,' Ellen said.

'That's true,' Jess said quietly.

'Peg, I have another idea. Would it be possible to meet with Amelia tomorrow, do you think?' Ellen asked.

'I would think so, she'll be at the shop all day.'

'Good, then it's settled. I'll pop over and have a word with her.'

The conversation then turned to Jess and Carter returning the stolen items and how she had managed to persuade the police to let them help.

'Jess, you never fail to amaze me!' Peg said, laughing. 'I can't believe you even suggested such a thing, let alone being given the job by the coppers.'

'Jess was adamant and the Detective Inspector really had no choice but to submit to her,' Carter said with a chuckle.

Peg noted the look of love which passed between the couple and her heart sang for her friend. After years of abuse, Jess Lacey was finally enjoying some happiness.

46

The following day, ledgers in hand, Jess and Carter went their separate ways. Dividing the work meant the task would take half the time and the sooner it was complete, the sooner they could concentrate on planning their wedding.

Leaving Enid and Bella in charge of the pub along with Gail, Ellen took the train to Wednesbury to meet with Peg and Amelia. Peg had already briefed her employer about the previous night's discussion and the pair were expecting Ellen's visit. Taking Ellen into the back room, Amelia served some refreshments and then the two women got down to business.

'Peg told me about your sister and I was sorry to hear it,' Ellen began. Amelia nodded her thanks. 'She also explained your offer to her of a partnership in the shop. As you may have suspected, Peg is not in a position, financially, to accept unless she has a sponsor.' Again Amelia nodded. 'Therefore, I'm here to see if you would be happy to share your longer-term plans. Are you for example looking to retire and move to Wales to be with your sister any time soon?'

'That's what I'd like to do. I've thought about selling the

shop but that seemed so unfair on Peg. She's been such a huge asset to the business, bringing in a lot of custom since she's been here. I'd also hate to disappoint our many loyal customers.'

'I offered to help Peg buy her share but that wouldn't help hasten your retirement,' Ellen pointed out. 'So, what I was wondering is – would you be prepared to sell your business to me?'

Amelia was surprised at the proposal. 'Well, that would certainly free me up to go to nurse my sister,' she said thoughtfully. 'Would you be promoting Peg to manager?'

'No, I plan to give a half share to Peg. Then when she's in a position to do so she can buy my half.'

'Crikey! That's incredibly generous of you, Ellen.'

'It seems to me that Peg deserves it,' Ellen said with a shrug.

'I agree with that sentiment. When did you have in mind for the sale and for what price?'

'If you're genuinely interested, let's have some more tea and we can thrash out the details,' Ellen suggested.

Peg, meanwhile, was bustling around, busy in the shop, all the time wondering what was being said between the two businesswomen in the back room.

* * *

Whilst discussions were underway in Wednesbury, Jess had taken a cab to an address in a wealthy part of Birmingham. The cabbie agreed to wait while Jess hammered on the knocker. Momentarily the door was opened by a young maid.

'Good morning, my name is Jess Lacey and I'm here to see Mr Fitzgerald.'

'Come in,' the maid said quietly. Closing the door, she went on, 'The master is in the study if you will follow me.'

Jess had the feeling the maid was not happy in her work; she had a frightened look about her which immediately put Jess on her guard.

Having been led into the study, Jess was faced with a young man sitting behind a huge desk. Jess introduced herself and then explained the reason for her visit. 'I believe you had a gold fob watch and chain stolen...'

'I did. Please take a seat. Would you care for tea, Miss Lacey?'

'Thank you but no.'

Mr Fitzgerald dismissed the maid with an arrogant flick of his hand. 'Now, about the watch and chain.'

Taking the items from her bag, Jess laid them on the desk. 'Are these the items you had stolen?'

'Indeed they are. How, may I ask, did you come by them?' he asked as his eyes roamed over her body.

Feeling distinctly uncomfortable, Jess was keen to be gone from this man's house. 'I am an assistant for the constabulary tasked with returning stolen property to the rightful owners,' Jess explained.

Fitzgerald laughed loudly. 'That's quite a story, Miss Lacey.'

Pulling out the letter of authority from the Detective Inspector, she passed it to him to read. Scanning the contents, he tossed it onto the desk. 'Forgive me if I don't believe a word of it, but that could have been written by anyone,' he scoffed.

'That's true enough, but you can always check with the sergeant at the station,' Jess replied.

Clearing his throat, Fitzgerald nodded. Letter secured away, Jess said, 'Please sign here as proof your items were received.' Jess pointed to the appropriate place in the open ledger.

Picking up a pen, Fitzgerald obliged then watched as Jess initialled next to his signature.

'Thank you, Mr Fitzgerald. I will bid you good day.' Jess got to her feet and strode from the room without waiting a moment longer.

The maid was hovering by the front door and Jess said quietly, 'If you should ever need help, find me at The Queen's Head public house. It's safe there. Just ask for Jess.'

'Thank you,' the maid whispered, fear written all over her face.

Jess climbed into the cab and called out the next address to visit. As the cab moved forward, Jess realised she was shaking. Mr Fitzgerald, although he had done nothing other than look at her in a leery way, had scared her. The feeling brought back the terror of living with an abusive husband, and Jess determined then and there that she and Carter should work together in future. It would take far longer to complete the job, but it would be much safer for her.

Trying to calm herself, Jess wondered how long it would be before she saw the maid again. Instinct told her it would be sooner rather than later.

After she had returned a silver snuff box to a Mrs Adcote, Jess hurried home to tell Gail about the possible new recruit to their number. Carter arrived back shortly after Jess. He was horrified to hear the tale of Fitzgerald and his lecherous looks, and he agreed they should go back to working as a pair from then onwards.

It was late in the day by the time Ellen came home and everyone was eager to know the outcome of her meeting with Amelia.

Raucous laughter came from the bar and Ellen raised her eyebrows.

'It's been like that all day,' Gail explained. 'Bella's telling jokes and the punters love it.'

Accepting the tea she had been offered, Ellen nodded with a grin. 'I have bought Amelia's shop,' she announced proudly.

A buzz of excitement ran around the kitchen as Jess, Carter and Gail congratulated Ellen on her new acquisition.

'When will you complete the transaction?' Jess asked.

'It's done. We went to a solicitor to have the paperwork drawn up and signed, and then to the bank for the money to be transferred.'

'What did Peg say?' Gail asked.

'She cried,' Ellen replied.

'Oh, no! Why?' Jess was worried for her friend.

'Because I had the deeds put in both our names. Peg is now part owner of Amelia's with the option to buy me out as and when she can afford it. Oh, and she has agreed to kit us all out for the wedding.'

'Ellen – I can't believe it!' Jess gushed. 'Thank you. Peg must be over the moon.'

'Pretty much,' Ellen said with a laugh.

More sombrely now, Jess told Ellen about her encounter with the frightened maid, and how she thought the girl would be coming to them soon.

'If she does that will be another saved from the clutches of a licentious brute,' Ellen said.

'There's no work for her here though, Ellen,' Gail put in.

'Maybe not, but Peg will need an assistant in the shop and I'm sure we can find her something.'

Clinking cups, the friends toasted to a good day all round.

47

It was just after breakfast when Jess received a visitor. Carter answered the knock on the door and led a young woman through to the kitchen, while Bella opened the bar to the public.

'I hope you don't mind me coming, but you said...'

'Of course I don't mind. Have a seat and tell us your name,' Jess encouraged the frightened-looking girl she'd met only the day before.

Gail poured her tea and then sat to listen, as did Jess, Ellen and Carter.

'My name is Hilda Francis.'

'I'm Jess, this is Ellen who owns the pub, Carter and Gail. Tell us your story, Hilda, don't be afraid because you're safe here with us.'

Hilda drew in a deep breath and began. 'I've been Mr Fitzgerald's maid for six months and I hate it – and him!'

Jess laid a comforting hand on Hilda's arm. 'Take your time.'

After a loud swallow, Hilda went on. 'He was nice to begin with, charming in fact. Then after a while he started to become over familiar with me.' Hilda's eyes dropped to the teacup in her hand.

'Has he...?' Ellen asked.

'No!' Hilda's head shot up. 'No, but I'm really scared it will come to that. Every day he gets bolder and yesterday he tried to kiss me.'

'Was that before my visit?' Jess asked. When Hilda nodded, she added, 'I guessed something was amiss straight away.'

'You said to come here if I needed help,' Hilda said, feeling afraid she might be turned away.

'You did the right thing. Now, do you have family locally?' Ellen asked.

'No, I was orphaned last year.'

'You poor lamb. I have a suggestion but first we have to get you out of Fitzgerald's employ. You will need to collect your things and...'

'I brought them with me,' Hilda interrupted, 'my bag is in the bar with the lady there. I made up my mind that even if you couldn't help me, I wasn't going back to Fitzgerald's.'

'All the better,' Ellen said. 'Jess, we're going to need Carol's room.'

'Of course, I'll go and prepare it right away. Carter, some help, please.'

'Hilda, you can stay with us for as long as you wish.' Ellen patted the girl's hand with a smile.

'I don't have much money,' Hilda said, reaching into her bag.

'You won't need it here,' Ellen assured her.

'Thank you so very much.' Hilda's eyes brimmed with tears.

'I might be able to secure you a job in a dress shop over in Wednesbury should the owner be agreeable,' Ellen said.

At that Hilda cried softly, feeling lucky to have happened upon these good people.

* * *

Hilda settled in very quickly, happily helping Gail in the kitchen preparing meals and washing dishes. After a few days, Ellen took Hilda to meet Peg with a view to finding her some work in the shop.

Peg greeted them both effervescently and Ellen explained Hilda's circumstances.

'I certainly could do with the help,' Peg said, 'but travelling back and forth every day would take up all of your wages.'

'Please don't turn me away, I'll work hard for you, I promise!' Hilda begged.

'I'm not turning you down, Hilda. When Amelia owned this place she lived here as well, so I propose you do the same.'

'That's a marvellous idea,' Ellen said.

'Forgive me for asking but don't you want to live here yourself, Mrs Butler?' Hilda asked.

'No, I like my house in Brick Kiln Croft. I wouldn't want to move now. Besides, this way I feel as though I'm *going out* to work. If I lived here it wouldn't feel much like home really.'

'I can understand that,' Hilda said.

'Good. Come on, I'll show you the living quarters.' Peg took them through to the back room which contained a settee and comfortable armchairs, a small table and a fireplace. This led to a kitchen and small scullery. Off the living room were stairs, at the top of which were two bedrooms; both had furniture and clean beds. Hilda looked out of the window onto an overgrown patch of land which housed the brick-built privy.

'This is lovely, Mrs Butler,' Hilda said.

'Call me Peg. If you want the job you can move in whenever you like.'

'I do! Yes, please and – thank you, Peg. I'll fetch my bag over later today.'

'That's settled then.' Peg beamed with pleasure at having hired her very first assistant, and at having saved the girl from having to live on the streets.

* * *

Over in Birmingham, Jess and Carter had set out together on yet another jaunt to return stolen goods.

'We're doing so well with all of this,' Jess said. 'I can hardly believe it.'

'I agree, I thought we would still be at it this time next year.'

'We need Sergeant Phillips to sign our ledgers today too, otherwise Detective Inspector Drake will be hunting us down.' Jess gave a little laugh.

'You are so beautiful, Jess, I adore you.' Carter grinned as their cab drew to a halt.

Once the lady of the house was happily reunited with her long-lost earrings, the cab ferried the couple to the police station.

Asking to see the sergeant, they waited while he was summoned.

'Well, well. I am delighted to see you both if only because it will get the Inspector off my back.'

'Hello, sergeant, we're here for your signature. I think you'll be pleased when you see the results of our undertaking,' Jess replied with a smile.

'Come through.' The sergeant ushered them into the little room where Jess and Carter passed the ledgers over.

Opening the books, the sergeant's eyes opened wide in

surprise. 'Will you look at that?' he said, 'I never would have believed it.'

'As you can see, we're almost finished,' Carter informed the sergeant. 'Anything we are unable to return we will bring to you along with the ledgers.'

'Very good. You've certainly made excellent progress.' The sergeant signed off the work completed, saying, 'Well done, both of you. You've saved my lads a lot of tiring legwork.'

'Which has allowed them to do such sterling jobs of catching criminals,' Jess added. Sergeant Phillips puffed out his chest at the compliment, pride written all over his face.

'Thank you, sergeant, we'd best get on with our work and leave you to yours,' Carter said, leading Jess out of the room.

Sergeant Phillips stood in the foyer of the police station, watching the couple board a cab. With a smile, he shook his head gently.

'Is there a problem, sergeant?' the duty constable asked from behind his desk.

'No, lad, no problem at all. I was just wishing there were more people like those two in the world.' With that he strode away, leaving the constable looking puzzled.

48

Jess and Carter worked hard to complete the mammoth task of returning jewellery and trinkets to their owners, with only a few items unaccounted for. The rolls of banknotes also remained unclaimed.

On a chilly Friday morning, the couple visited the police station for the last time. As usual they were shown into the little room by Sergeant Phillips, who duly signed the ledgers.

Then in strode Detective Inspector Drake. 'Ah, now I see why I was sent for,' he said, eyeing the couple who sat at the small table.

'Miss Lacey and Mr Adams have finished their assignment, sir.'

Drake checked the books then looked up in astonishment. 'Congratulations. I have to admit I had my doubts in the beginning, but the sergeant had faith in you and your intentions and he was proved right.'

Jess cringed inwardly at the back-handed compliment as she placed the letters of authorisation on the table. 'The money we couldn't match to anyone, of course, and you'll find it's all there in the box,' she said.

'Erm... sir, I don't rightly see how we could keep that cash. It could be misconstrued as us taking a bribe or stealing it for our own use.' Sergeant Phillips waited to see what the Inspector would answer.

'It's evidence, sergeant,' came the reply.

'I see that, sir, but it's as Mrs Lacey said, we can't be sure who it belongs to.'

After a moment's thought, the Inspector said, 'Quite right, sergeant. I suggest it be given over as a reward for a job well done. What say you?'

'I agree, sir.'

Jess and Carter exchanged a look of surprise when the Inspector handed the money to them. 'Well deserved, I'm sure,' the Inspector said.

'Shouldn't it go to Mr Frith?' Jess asked.

'That money could have come from anywhere, Mrs Lacey, how would you suggest we trace it back?'

'Well, obviously I can't...'

'Then take it as payment for a job very well done.'

'Thank you so very much!' Jess said.

They were led out of the room and were about to leave the station when they had to move aside when two constables hauled a struggling man into the foyer.

'Ah now, you have the wrong man, so you do.'

'Is that right?' one policeman said.

'To be sure. I don't frequent the basin area.'

Jess's ears pricked up and she glanced at Carter.

'Look, mate, you were recognised.'

'By who?'

'Whom,' the constable corrected.

'Not by one of them prostitutes!' the man said.

'Those prostitutes.'

Corrected again, the man exhaled loudly.

'No one said anything about a lady of the night,' the other policeman pointed out, 'so how would you know about them if you hadn't been there?' Then to the duty officer he said, 'Book him in.'

'What for?'

'Suspected murder. We found this knife on him and there's still blood on it.'

'I ain't done nothin'!' the man raged as he fought the policemen in an attempt to get away.

The constable who had corrected his speech yelled, 'I haven't done anything!' Then, out of patience, he bunched his fist and hit the man on the jaw. The effect was immediate as the fellow crumpled at the knees.

Jess and Carter exchanged a shocked look before stepping outside. 'I wonder if that's the man who assaulted Enid,' Carter said.

'Who knows, but I'm sure she'll be delighted to hear someone has been arrested,' Jess said.

Jess and Carter were considerably richer when they left the station than when they went in. 'This helps to cover all the cab fares we spent,' Carter said.

Jess nodded. 'I'm amazed, Carter. All this money given to us just like that!' she said, snapping her fingers.

'We more than earned it, Jess,' he pointed out. 'And as you said previously, the money could belong to anyone. It would be impossible to link it with any one person.'

'I suppose so, I was just taken aback at the simplicity of the decision.'

'Me too if I'm honest,' he said. 'Jess, now can we plan our wedding?'

With a grin, Jess nodded. 'Nothing would give me more pleasure.'

On their return to The Queen's Head, Jess and Carter did that very thing, sitting in the kitchen discussing everything, from the order of service to the menu for their bridal feast. Jess couldn't ever remember being this happy.

When Carter returned to his work and with nothing more to do to help the police, Jess realised she missed working the bar. Bella and Enid had it running smoothly and were loving their new jobs. Jess knew if she took over once more then the women would be forced back out onto the streets and she couldn't allow that to happen. But, having had a taste of working for a living, Jess knew she would never be content being just a housewife again. It was something she needed to discuss with Carter and she worried about his reaction.

Carter was surprised when Jess raised the subject one night after lock-up.

'I hadn't given it a thought,' he confessed.

'I know we don't need the money but I can't sit around doing nothing,' Jess admitted.

'Nor should you,' Ellen agreed. 'What sort of work do you want?'

'I loved the bar but I refuse to push Bella and Enid out because of my selfish desires.'

'Why not buy a pub of your own?' Ellen suggested. 'The two of you could run one easily enough if you hired some staff.'

'It's a thought,' Carter said in answer to Jess's questioning look.

'I think it's a great idea, although I'd miss you,' Gail added.

'How would we find a public house for sale?' Jess asked.

'Contact the Midland Brewery on Nova Scotia Street. They might be able to help because they supply most of the pubs in town,' Ellen offered helpfully. 'They will know of any up for sale. I'll be doing the rounds of my other pubs tomorrow so I'll ask around, maybe the managers might have heard of somewhere up for sale.'

'It's something to think about for sure,' Jess nodded, 'for after the wedding though. I'm going to see Peg tomorrow about my gown.'

Carter breathed a sigh of relief that Jess was putting their marriage ceremony first. He'd begun to worry that her search for work might delay it somehow and he was desperate to make her his wife. He watched quietly as his betrothed excitedly chatted about dresses, flowers, food and the honeymoon and he realised he'd never been this happy. The woman he adored was about to become his wife and, God willing, would make him a father. And to top it all, they were considering sinking their reward money into a business venture which would secure their future into old age.

Jess was thinking much the same thing as she listened to Gail's menu ideas. There was nothing that could mar the joy she was feeling at that moment.

* * *

Early the next morning, Jess boarded the train for Wednesbury. She was hoping Peg would assist her in choosing a design for her wedding gown. Decadently, she travelled first class again. Enjoying coffee and cake as clouds of steam rushed past the window when the train pulled out, Jess considered her options: tulle, chiffon or silk? All were beautiful; and then there was a choice of flowers. She wondered what would be available now winter was almost upon them.

The journey was swift and leaving the train and station, Jess caught a cab to Amelia's. *Will Peg change the name of the shop now that she's part owner?* she thought.

Greeted warmly by her good friend and the assistant, Hilda, Jess explained her reason for the visit. 'I'm going to need a lot of help,' she said as she took a seat.

'So am I if I'm to outfit you lot,' Peg replied with a grin. 'I will have to find a couple of good seamstresses.'

'Oh, Peg, that will cost! I didn't think about that aspect.'

'The business is doing well enough to afford it, Jess. Hilda is a marvel and clothes are flying out of the door.'

'I'm glad to hear it. Carter and I have been thinking of buying our own pub after we're wed.'

'That's good news. I'm sure you'll do great. Now let's get down to the reason you're here – your gown.'

As they talked, Hilda showed Jess some dress patterns and Jess quickly chose one. Lace bodice with a high neck and long sleeves attached to a silk skirt, the back of which lay over a small bustle. Simple but elegant and Jess was delighted. Peg took her measurements, which Hilda jotted down next to the sketch.

'I expect Ellen, Gail, Bella and Enid will be over to see you in the next few days too,' Jess said.

'What about Carter?'

'I don't know, he might want to go to a tailor.'

'I can understand that. He could feel awkward being measured up for trousers by us,' Peg said with a cheeky grin.

'I'm not sure about flowers.'

'White roses,' Hilda suggested.

'Would they be in season?' Jess asked.

'You pay enough and the florist can get whatever you want,' Hilda assured her.

By the time she left, Jess was feeling much more organised and like the wedding plans were finally coming together, especially as Carter should, at that moment, be discussing a date with the vicar of St Bart's.

On arriving home, Jess learned she was to be wed on 10 December and immediately she flew into a panic – how would everything be ready in time?

Gail sat her friend down with a strong cup of tea, the remedy for everything.

'I've decided to have one of those new-fangled telephones installed,' Ellen informed them. 'All this dashing about just to speak to someone is a thing of the past.'

'That's a splendid idea,' Carter said. 'It will help with the ordering from the brewery.'

* * *

It was happenstance that over in Wednesbury Peg was actually organising the very same thing. Her telephone would be fitted in the shop as soon as the telecom company were able and once that was sorted, Peg moved on to the Servants' Registry with a request for two seamstresses, preferably with experience in tailoring for men.

Over the next few days, Peg would be surprised by the number of women applying for the jobs. It appeared more and more women were looking for work – whether it was because they were desperate for the money or they were taking their lives into their own hands rather than be beholden to their husbands, Peg had no idea. What she did know was there were many talented people finally wanting to take the first step into the working world.

49

Jess and Carter took over the bar on the day Bella and Enid went to Amelia's to get fitted. Both found outfits on the rails that they fell in love with, although Bella's needed adjusting to fit her larger frame. Enid chose a blue wool jacket and skirt and Bella went for a dress in green.

Whilst they were at the dress shop, Jess was enjoying her time serving drinks, which only confirmed her need to have a pub of her own alongside her husband. They had discussed the idea whenever they had a spare moment, and both agreed they wanted to take on the responsibility of being employers rather than be employed by another. They were grateful to Ellen, of course, for not only taking them in but also teaching them everything she knew about running a pub.

Ellen's telephone was installed and was being used for brewery orders as well as supplies from the grocer and butcher. She was delighted at not having to run around town at last and could spend her time visiting her other premises, all of which were doing well.

Meanwhile, Gail had suggested hot and cold food for the reception after the wedding, as people would be in need of warmth after walking back from the church. A cold buffet where folk could help themselves and hot stew could be served to those who wanted it. She would make fresh bread and homemade dumplings as well as pork pies, sandwiches, pickles and anything else Jess needed.

The time came when Ellen and Gail were next to visit Amelia's to choose an outfit. Ellen opted for a burgundy wool suit, and Gail lifted a dress of blush pink from the rail. After a try-on session, both were more than happy with their choices.

Carter, as everyone thought he would, decided to buy a suit from a gents' tailor, complete with top hat, tails and cravat. He shyly admitted he wasn't comfortable at being measured up by a woman and was pleasantly surprised when everyone said they understood.

Jess ordered white roses for her bouquet and was happy that everything was in order. She was sure she had thought of everything until one evening when Ellen asked, 'Who will give you away?'

The colour drained from Jess's face. 'Jim, I hope.'

'You haven't asked him, have you?'

'No, I... forgot.'

'Ring Peg at the shop tomorrow and ask her to ask him on your behalf,' Ellen instructed. 'Now, Carter, who is your best man?'

'I don't have one,' he replied.

'Jess, also ask if one of Jim's pals will stand for Carter.'

Gail sat at the table with the others and asked, 'Will you move into Carter's room once you're wed?'

Where Jess had paled a moment ago, now her face flushed red. 'I... erm...' She looked around for help.

'I think it would be a good idea.' Carter came to the rescue and Jess smiled her appreciation.

'That's everything then,' Ellen said, 'now we wait until the big day.'

* * *

Over the next weeks, the weather turned colder. The mornings were frosty, and a very weak sun tried her best to shine on the humans bustling about beneath her. Overcoats, boots and mufflers were donned by the wealthy, and thick shawls or jackets had to suffice for the poor.

Jess's gown was delivered by Hilda who enjoyed tea and a catch-up with everyone. The gown was immediately hidden away until the big day dawned.

Jim had said Harry would be best man for Carter and it would be his honour to give the bride away.

Two days before the wedding, the residents of Birmingham awoke to a white world. Snow had fallen silently throughout the night and lay in thick layers everywhere. With a dressing gown wrapped around her, Jess breathed on her window and rubbed away the melted ice. Through the peephole, she gazed upon the street, unable to tell road from path.

'Oh, Lord!' she whispered as she quickly dressed, had a wash, brushed her teeth then ran downstairs for breakfast.

The kitchen was welcoming with its warmth and the aroma of cooking bacon tickled her taste buds.

'Have you seen the snow?' Jess asked.

'Yes, and before you start to panic I'm sure it will be gone by Saturday,' Gail said, cracking eggs into a massive frying pan.

'I do hope so,' Jess said.

'Stop fretting and cut some bread for frying in the bacon liquor.'

Carter and Ellen appeared from upstairs, both shivering. 'We need to light the fire in the bar,' Ellen said.

'Tea's in the pot and breakfast is almost ready,' Gail informed them, 'then we can worry about the bar.'

* * *

Over in Wednesbury, it was cold but as yet no snow had fallen. The locals glanced at the sky, however, knowing it was coming. Hilda had opened the shop and Peg rushed in, feeling frozen.

'Hot coffee,' Hilda said, holding out a cup.

'You treasure!' Peg took the drink, blew on the surface and sipped. 'It'll be a bugger getting to Birmingham on Saturday if we get the snow,' Peg said.

'The trains will still run though, won't they?'

'I hope so, cocka, otherwise we'll have to walk it 'cos the cabs won't be any good.'

The bell tinkled and Hilda said, 'I'll go, you sit by the fire and get warm.'

* * *

Fortunately no snow fell on Wednesbury and by the weekend a thaw had taken place in Birmingham. On the morning of the wedding, Jess stayed in her room. To see her betrothed before the ceremony was to invite bad luck, so Gail took a breakfast tray to her friend. She found Jess sitting on the bed, staring into space.

'Jess?' she enquired, laying the tray on the dressing table.

'I was just thinking,' Jess said quietly.

'What, love?'

'About everything since I came here to escape Bill's abuse, and how you were all so kind to me. Bill's death and the secret we all carry around to keep Jim safe. Learning to work the bar and Kathy's hatred of me. Her demise and then returning all the things she had stolen. Now I'm getting married again.'

'You're not having second thoughts, are you?'

'No. It's just that such a lot has happened in such a short time. Carter and I have been so busy we haven't had a courtship as such.'

'He adores you, Jess, that's all that matters,' Gail said, sitting next to her friend.

'I know and I love him so much, but I wonder if we are rushing things.'

'This is nothing more than pre-wedding nerves. Have your breakfast and then I'll do your hair.'

'Thank you, I expect you're right.' Jess smiled and went to pour tea while Gail sorted out hair pins.

'I'll come back when I've seen the others off to the church. Jim will be here soon.' Gail left Jess to her food and rushed downstairs.

Jim had in fact arrived and the kitchen was bustling and busy, with everyone speaking at once. 'Gail, the cabs are here,' Jim informed her.

'Right. Bella, Enid and Ellen, off you go. I'll follow along once I've helped Jess into her gown.' She ushered the excited women out to their transport. To Jim she asked, 'Where's Peg?'

'At the church already.'

'Good. Have yourself a cuppa while I dress the bride,' she said before dashing back upstairs.

Gail pinned Jess's hair up and set it with white rose buds,

then helped Jess into her gown. 'You look beautiful!' Gail gasped as she handed Jess her bouquet.

The friends shared a hug before descending the stairs.

'Blimey, look at you!' Jim said with a grin, holding out a coat for Jess to slip into.

'Come on, your cab's waiting and I have to lock up,' Gail urged.

Taking Jim's arm, Jess drew in a breath. She was about to start a whole new chapter of her life, and an excited shudder ran down her spine.

Gail arrived at St Bart's just before Jess and Jim and she hurried inside to take her seat. She smiled and nodded at Carter, who was waiting with his best man, Harry, in front of the vicar.

The organ struck up and the small congregation, comprising Gail, Ellen, Peg, Hilda, George, Harry and Bert with their wives, as well as the seamstresses hired by Peg, along with Mr Appleby, the neighbour from Brick Kiln Croft, stood and turned to watch the bride's entrance. A church assistant took Jess's coat and Jess smiled her thanks. There were gasps at how lovely Jess looked and Peg dabbed her eyes with her handkerchief.

When Jess reached her betrothed, she saw tears in his eyes. With a reassuring smile, she turned to face the vicar.

'Dearly beloved...' The words carried to the back of the church. The wedding had begun.

50

The solitary bell rang out as Mr and Mrs Adams left the church. Well-wishers had gathered on the grounds and the street where the cabs were lined up waiting for their passengers. A chimney sweep stepped forward to shake hands with the happy couple in the time-honoured tradition of bringing them good luck.

'Well, Mrs Adams, how do you feel?' Carter asked.

'Very happy, Mr Adams,' Jess replied as they walked along the gravel path.

The convoy of cabs made their way back to The Queen's Head where they disgorged their fares before moving off to find more work.

Indoors, Bella opened the bar for the wedding guests and Gail got busy with the food. Hilda made hot tea and Peg and Ellen sat at the table discussing the church service.

'It was so nice of you to invite me, Mrs Lacey... oh, sorry, Mrs Adams,' Mr Appleby said as he sought out Jess amongst the throng of bodies.

'You are most welcome, Mr Appleby, I'm glad you could

come. I'll always be grateful that you helped save Peg that day, you're a hero.'

The old man smiled and hobbled to the bar for a beer.

Jess and Carter helped Gail unwrap the plates of food, revealing pork pies, pickles, ham on the bone, slices of roast beef, game pie, cheeses and freshly baked bread. A huge pot of broth simmered gently on the hotplate of the range.

Harry, Bert and George and their wives were in the bar with Bella and Enid enjoying pints of beer for the men and gin for the ladies. Jim stood in the doorway watching his pals to his left, and the others in the kitchen to his right. Then his eyes found his wife, who was now hugging Jess, a smile lighting up her face. He could so easily have lost her at the hands of Bill Lacey, but he hadn't. Once again he silently thanked God for His mercy in saving his wife.

'Remember when you left Brick Kiln Croft and you gave me your wedding ring to sell?' Peg asked Jess. At her nod Peg went on, 'Well this is what I got for it.' Peg handed over the money she'd been keeping for her friend.

'Thank you, Peg,' Jess said as she wrapped her arms around the woman who was like a sister to her.

The food was consumed along with copious amounts of alcohol. Bella had everyone roaring with laughter at her jokes and then Jess was asked to sing. Silence descended as her voice rang out clear and true. After thunderous applause, Bella encouraged the whole room to join in the next song.

Eventually, late into the night, the party began to wind down. The guests said their goodbyes and departed, and the clean-up began. With all hands to the pump, the pub was tidy in no time.

Gail and Ellen went to bed, leaving Carter and Jess alone in the warm kitchen.

'You're very quiet, sweetheart,' Carter said.

'Am I?' Jess replied timidly.

'What's wrong, my love? Please don't tell me you're regretting...'

'No! I'm glad we're wed. It's just... I'm – nervous.' Jess flushed scarlet and lowered her eyes.

'Oh, darlin', you don't have to be. Nothing will happen until you are ready, I swear.'

Jess sighed with relief. It had been a long time since she had been loved as a woman rather than abused against her will, and she fretted that Carter would be disappointed in her.

'You go up while I secure the doors and make everything safe,' he encouraged.

Jess nodded. At the top of the stairs, she halted and looked back. This was where Kathy Frith had died after falling in a drunken stupor. Shaking off the thought, Jess stepped into Carter's room. She felt like she was trespassing and just stood there. Hearing Carter's tread behind her, she shivered.

'I'll light the fire while you get into bed,' he whispered.

Jess saw her nightgown laid out ready for her and she smiled at Gail's thoughtfulness. She quickly changed and climbed under the covers, dithering from the cold.

Carter had a roaring fire going in minutes and the dancing flames gave comfort as well as warmth. Washing his hands in the bowl on the dresser, he then began to undress.

Suddenly feeling very shy, Jess averted her eyes. Turning out the light, Carter then climbed in beside her. Holding out his arm, he smiled as Jess snuggled into him.

With the eiderdown up to their chins, they watched the light from the crackling fire dance across the ceiling.

'I love you, Jess,' he whispered.

'I love you too,' she replied. As they kissed, Jess felt the fire in her veins rushing around her body, and she no longer felt shy or afraid. She gave herself to her husband freely and with all of her heart.

* * *

Over breakfast the following morning, Ellen said, 'You two should have a honeymoon. It would do you good to get away somewhere nice, by the seaside perhaps.'

'It's a nice idea, but I'd rather we put our money into buying our own pub. What do you think, Carter?' Jess asked.

'I agree. We'll need every penny if we're to have our own business.'

'I've been thinking about that. Why not buy one of mine?' Jess gaped at Ellen's offer. 'I tell you what, I'll take you to see them and if you like one of them we can draw up the paperwork. I don't have the time or energy I used to and spend most of my days here at The Queen's Head. You'd be doing me a favour really.'

'That would be marvellous,' Jess said, 'but your managers won't be pleased at the idea, I'm sure.'

'It's not down to them. Besides, the manager at the Old Red Lion on the Bull Ring is looking to get out of the pub trade. He's only there while I find a replacement.'

'Maybe we should look at that one then,' Carter said.

Wrapped up against the cold, the three took a cab to a huge building that stood on the crossroads of St Martin's Lane, Digbeth and the Bull Ring. Across the way was St Martin's church rectory, and behind the pub was a hotel.

Paying the cabbie, Ellen led Jess and Carter inside. Even this early in the morning the bar was packed with night workers coming off shifts. The roaring fire in the large grate kept the customers warm as they talked, laughed and drank.

Going through to the back room, Ellen introduced Jess and Carter to the manager, Eli Watkins, and the cook, May Butterworth. There were two young men tending the bar – supposedly, but Jess noted they were chatting more than serving.

'I'm going to show Jess and Carter around because they could be interested in buying the place,' Ellen explained.

'Just to let you know, Ernie brought in another young woman last night,' Eli said.

'Oh, where is she now?' Ellen asked.

'She fled again after breakfast. She was petrified of something – or someone,' Eli explained. 'I couldn't get her to stay.'

'All right, thanks, Eli,' Ellen said. 'I'll go and check on the other pubs in the next few days and see how they're faring.' Turning to Jess and Carter, she went on, 'We'll start through here.'

The back room was cosy and warm and led onto a large kitchen and scullery. Another room served as a parlour of sorts. The cellar was massive and dry, although in need of a coat of whitewash. Barrels were stacked neatly and rows of shelves contained boxes loaded with bottles of spirits. Carter was impressed and said so. Upstairs there were five bedrooms and an indoor bathroom; the whole place was lit by electricity which showed up the poor décor.

'It needs some work, as you can see,' Ellen said. 'Once decorated, the rooms could be let out on a nightly basis, or be used by staff. Only one is occupied at present by Eli. May comes in to cook then she goes home to take care of her sick mother.'

Going back downstairs, they checked out the bar again. It was then that Jess saw one of the barmen ring up the till but slide the money into his pocket.

'He's stealing from you, Ellen,' Jess whispered, 'I saw him.'

'Really? Well, I'm not having that!'

'Wait, just watch and see if he does it again,' Jess suggested.

Sure enough, a while later the barman did indeed pocket a coin and then, unbelievably, he gave the change from the till.

'Well, I never! The cheek of him!' Ellen gasped. Then she called the young man into the kitchen where she had him empty his pockets.

'What the hell is going on?' he asked.

'I saw you stealing money so – you're fired!' Ellen snapped. 'Get your coat and leave my pub.'

To his credit, the young man did just that without causing a fuss. He had been caught redhanded and he knew it so there was no point in denying it.

'Other than that thieving bugger, what do you think of the place?'

Jess and Carter exchanged a look and a nod. 'I love it!' Jess said.

'So do I,' Carter concurred.

'Let's go home and discuss the details then,' Ellen said. 'Eli, you're on the bar because I've just sacked one of your barmen for stealing.'

They walked out, leaving Eli Watkins with a shocked look on his face.

51

Back at The Queen's Head, they were surprised to see Gail tending the bar.

'Where are Bella and Enid?' Ellen asked.

'Down the police station.'

'What's happened?' Jess questioned, looking worried.

'Enid has been asked to an identification parade to see if she can pick out the fella who battered her. She didn't want to go on her own so Bella went with her. They should be back shortly.'

'I wonder if it's the same man who we saw arrested that day,' Jess said.

'We'll find out soon enough,' Carter replied.

Jess and Carter took over the bar, releasing Gail to her kitchen once more.

About an hour later, Bella and Enid returned and informed everyone that Enid had indeed picked out the man who had assaulted her. 'The coppers are taking him to court for murder!' Enid said.

'I can't believe how lucky you were that night, Enid,' Jess

said. 'It's my belief he thought he had killed you and so he fled the scene.'

'Ar, well, he's behind bars now and he'll be staying there a bloody long time!' Bella put in.

Jess and Carter then went to Ellen's office where discussions of the selling and buying of the Old Red Lion took place.

'Are you sure this is what you both want?' Ellen asked.

Jess nodded. 'It's time, Ellen. We will always be grateful for everything you've done for us, but we both agree we need to do this. Providing, of course, that we can afford it.'

The finer details were discussed and once agreed, Ellen immediately went to her solicitor to have the paperwork drawn up. The documents would be signed by all involved and witnessed by the solicitor. Following that, she informed the bank of the imminent sale, and who would be taking over the property.

Going to the sign-writers, she ordered a new sign for over the door. *Proprietors, Carter and Jess Adams.* She hoped her friends would be happy with her choice and didn't feel like she was interfering.

Inside a week, the papers were signed, each being given a copy, a new account at the bank was set up, and Mr and Mrs Adams took charge of their new business venture. 'I can't believe how quickly it's all been done,' Jess said one evening. 'Tomorrow we move into our new home.'

'I'm going to miss you,' Gail said tearfully.

'Me too, but we can visit each other anytime,' Jess said. 'Ellen, I can't thank you enough for everything you've done for me.'

'Enjoy your life, Jess, that will be thanks enough.'

* * *

The following day, Jess and Carter said their goodbyes and boarded a cab with their luggage. They were both excited at the prospect of running their own pub, but sad to be leaving their friends.

On arrival at the Old Red Lion, they took their cases to the room they had chosen between them and unpacked. Then they went to the kitchen, where May provided tea and cake.

Eli was paid his final wages and happily left the pub and when the other young barman arrived he was also paid off when Carter explained they needed their staff to work, not stand around chatting.

A notice was put in the window advertising that bar staff were needed.

Whilst May prepared lunch, Jess familiarised herself with the bar. Not happy with the layout, she began to move bottles and glasses to more accessible places. Meanwhile, Carter was in the cellar checking stock and the order sheets along with the prices.

The pub remained closed during the morning while Jess and Carter settled in. May provided a thick hot stew and dumplings and fresh bread for lunch.

'May, I'm thinking we could use you full time here at the pub,' Jess said.

'I can't, Mrs Adams, my old mum is poorly and I have to see to her.'

'I'm sorry to hear that.'

'I'll understand if'n you need to get yourself a new cook,' May said sadly.

'No, it was just an idea. I don't wish to replace you,' Jess replied quickly. 'Do you have far to go to get home?'

'Ar, a fair way. I rent a house over in Bartholomew Row over the back of the church.'

'That must be expensive in cab fares,' Jess said.

'I can't afford that, Mrs Adams, I walk.'

'Oh, I see.' Jess looked at Carter and was surprised when he nodded.

'May, first of all I'm Carter and this is Jess and we'd be pleased if you would address us as such. Now, if I'm reading my wife's mind correctly, I'm sure she's thinking to offer you and your mother a room here so you don't have all that walking to do twice a day.'

'That's exactly what I had in mind!' Jess said, beaming at her new husband.

'Oh, Mr... Carter, do you really mean it?'

'I do, and if your mother agrees then the sooner the better.'

'Mum would love it. She gets lonely when I'm working and I think that's half the problem with her health.'

'All right, after lunch take a cab home and bring your mother back with you. That way she can decide for herself,' Jess suggested.

In her excitement, May finished her lunch in quick-smart time.

'May, take some of that stew for your mum because it's delicious,' Jess praised.

When the cook had left, Jess went to sit on Carter's knee, her arms about his neck. 'Thank you for that,' she said.

'I guessed what you were thinking – and rightly it seems. It makes sense all round.'

'Let's see what happens when they come back but I have a feeling it will turn out well.' With that, Jess kissed the man she loved with all her heart.

Jess was correct about the happy outcome – May and her mother, Bess, did indeed love the idea of living at the pub. In fact, May moved them in that very afternoon while Jess and

Carter opened the bar for business. Mother and daughter had little in the way of belongings so the move went smoothly enough. Bess sat at the kitchen table while May worked and she was soon helping chop vegetables. Clearly Bess's illness was nothing more than old age and loneliness.

By the time Carter locked up for the night, everyone was tired, but nonetheless tea was drunk as they all got to know each other.

'Who did the cleaning here?' Jess asked.

'Eli was supposed to but he didn't bother much,' May replied.

'We'll need to hire someone then,' Carter said.

That night, four people slept in their new home, happy and content.

* * *

Over the next week, the Adamses employed a cleaner and two young barmen. The Old Red Lion now had a full complement of staff, and the drinkers came in droves to meet the new owners.

Jess had a telephone installed to help with brewery orders as well as having a quick catch-up with Peg, Ellen and Gail, and after the first six months of business Jess and Carter were able to show a healthy profit, and much to the workers' delight, they gave each a rise in wages.

It was around this time that Jess began to feel ill. She tired quickly and her stomach rebelled whenever she ate anything. The weather was hot and steamy and Jess thought she had caught a chill or contracted a tummy bug. She struggled to keep food down and even felt sick after a drink of water. She tried her best to continue working but found she was exhausted, which was making her tearful and depressed.

One morning, Bess took her aside. 'You, my girl, should see the doctor because it's my guess that you'm with child.'

Jess was shocked. 'I don't think so, I couldn't conceive in my previous marriage. My late husband always said I was barren.'

Bess sighed loudly. 'Bloody men, what do they know about the workings of a woman's body? When was your last monthly?'

Jess thought for a moment. 'I can't remember!'

'There you go then. Take my advice and go get checked out.'

'I will, Bess, thank you. In fact, I'll go now if you don't mind, but don't tell anyone else, I don't want Carter to worry. I'll call in at the market on the way back as an excuse for being out.'

Grabbing her bag and a basket, Jess slipped out of the back door and hailed a cab. She felt excited at the prospect of being pregnant, but if she wasn't then there was something really wrong with her. She tried not to dwell on that thought but she couldn't push it away either.

At her destination, Jess paid the cabbie and rang the bell of the doctor's surgery. After being given admittance by a receptionist, Jess took a seat to wait to be seen.

Walking around the market an hour later, Jess couldn't believe what she'd been told. The doctor confirmed that she was pregnant, around five months gone, he guessed. Barely able to concentrate on her shopping, Jess took a cab home. She was tired and her legs and back ached.

Bess was waiting in the kitchen when Jess walked in. She raised her eyebrows in question and Jess smiled. Bess nodded once and set the kettle to boil as Jess placed the basket on the table.

Carter came up from the cellar and moved to kiss his wife. 'Been shopping?'

'Hmm,' Jess said, bursting with happiness. 'Sweetheart, I have some news.'

'Good news, I hope,' he replied.

'The best.' Jess pulled a package from the basket on the table and unwrapped it. A pair of tiny white knitted booties lay on her outstretched hand.

Carter's mouth fell open in surprise then with a wide grin on his countenance he hugged his wife. 'Jess, my love, you've made me the happiest of men. Thank you!'

Bess and May gave their congratulations and a moment later Carter rushed through to the bar. 'I'm going to be a father!' he yelled. Applause and whistles resounded and Jess sat at the table, shaking her head at his antics.

'You were right, Bess – bloody men!' Jess said with a laugh.

Bess and May joined in the joviality before Bess said, 'You'll do all the work and he'll get the pats on the back.'

'As with all things, Bess, it's a man's world, after all.'

'You reckon? They wouldn't get very far without us to have all the babbies!'

'Wise words, Mum,' May said.

'I ain't just a pretty face, you know,' Bess smiled.

Amid the laughter, Jess gave silent thanks to the Almighty for bringing her so much joy in her life. She'd walked a hard road to get to this point and had survived; she was now ready to face anything life could throw at her.

In the next few months she would become a mother, something she never thought could happen, and she was deliriously happy.

Once she had shared the news with Peg, Gail and Ellen, Jess decided she would begin planning for the baby's arrival. There was a lot to do in a short time but as with everything Jess Adams took on, she was determined to rise to the challenge.

She had a wonderful husband who adored her, as well as good friends around her. There was nothing Jess couldn't tackle now, even the pain of childbirth. A whole new chapter of her life had opened before her, and Jess Adams was ready to welcome it with open arms.

* * *

MORE FROM LINDSEY HUTCHINSON

ABOUT THE AUTHOR

Lindsey Hutchinson is a bestselling saga author whose novels include *The Workhouse Children*. She was born and raised in Wednesbury, and was always destined to follow in the footsteps of her mother, the multi-million selling Meg Hutchinson.

Download your exclusive bonus content from Lindsey Hutchinson here:

Follow Lindsey on social media:

x.com/LHutchAuthor

bookbub.com/authors/lindsey-hutchinson

ALSO BY LINDSEY HUTCHINSON

The Children from Gin Barrel Lane

Minnie's Orphans

The Hat Girl From Silver Street

A Winter Baby for Gin Barrel Lane

The Runaway Children

The Hat Girl's Heartbreak

The Ragged Orphan

The Bad Penny

The Orphan's Promise

The Girl from The Queen's Head

The Pick-Pocket Series

The Pick-Pocket Orphans

The Pick-Pocket's Plight

The Pick-Pocket's Return

www.ingramcontent.com/pod-product-compliance
Ingram Content Group UK Ltd.
Pitfield, Milton Keynes, MK11 3LW, UK
UKHW011328110526
12398UKWH00032B/733

9 781835 189290